SHOWDOWN
ON THE JUBILEE

Also by L. P. Holmes
in Large Print:

Apache Desert
Bloody Saddles
The Distant Vengeance
Flame of Sunset
High Starlight
Night Marshal
The Plunderers
Rustler's Moon
The Savage Hours
Somewhere They Die
Catch and Saddle
Desert Rails
Payoff at Pawnee
Shadow of the Rim

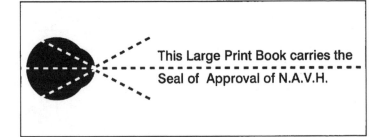

SHOWDOWN
ON THE JUBILEE

L. P. HOLMES

Thorndike Press • Waterville, Maine

Published in 2005 by arrangement with
Golden West Literary Agency.

Thorndike Press® Large Print Western.

The tree indicium is a trademark of Thorndike Press.

The text of this Large Print edition is unabridged.
Other aspects of the book may vary from the original edition.

Set in 16 pt. Plantin.

Printed in the United States on permanent paper.

Library of Congress Cataloging-in-Publication Data

Holmes, L. P. (Llewellyn Perry), 1895–
    Showdown on the Jubilee / by L. P. Holmes.
        p. cm. — (Thorndike Press large print westerns)
    ISBN 0-7862-7922-2 (lg. print : hc : alk. paper)
    1. Ranchers — Fiction. 2. Cattle stealing — Fiction.
3. Large type books. I. Title. II. Thorndike Press large
print Western series.
    PS3515.O4448S56 2005
    813′.52—dc22   2005014748

SHOWDOWN
ON THE JUBILEE

As the Founder/CEO of NAVH, the only national health agency solely devoted to those who, although not totally blind, have an eye disease which could lead to serious visual impairment, I am pleased to recognize Thorndike Press* as one of the leading publishers in the large print field.

Founded in 1954 in San Francisco to prepare large print textbooks for partially seeing children, NAVH became the pioneer and standard setting agency in the preparation of large type.

Today, those publishers who meet our standards carry the prestigious "Seal of Approval" indicating high quality large print. We are delighted that Thorndike Press is one of the publishers whose titles meet these standards. We are also pleased to recognize the significant contribution Thorndike Press is making in this important and growing field.

Lorraine H. Marchi, L.H.D.
Founder/CEO
NAVH

* Thorndike Press encompasses the following imprints: Thorndike, Wheeler, Walker and Large Print Press.

CHAPTER

I

The two-year-old whiteface steer lay dead in a small meadow in the timber, the gather of buzzards that had signaled Dave Howison to this spot still circling above. In their eagerness, some of these somber-coated scavengers swooped so low the rush of air through their curving, outstretched pinions produced a thinly vibrant hum, and their wheeling shadows made shifting patterns across the meadow's tawny, late-summer grass.

A swarm of green flies buzzed about the carcass, and for a little time Howison studied the dead animal from the vantage point of his saddle. Then, as the implications of what occurred struck more solidly, he swung down and moved up on foot for a closer examination. The white face had been slow-elked, and wastefully so. Only a loin and a quarter, raggedly chopped out, had been taken. The remainder of the critter lay on its near side, hiding the brand. A smear of blackened blood from a bullet hole between its eyes told how the luckless brute had died.

Howison straightened and looked around. Aside from the carcass at his feet and the grisly birds of carrion soaring impatiently above, there was nothing suspicious in the visible surroundings. Past the edges of the meadow the sun-drenched timber marched, its warm, resinous breath pungent but pleasant in a man's nostrils. Somewhere out there a pine squirrel, cutting cones, set up a brief scolding. But the sound, small and of little consequence, was soon absorbed by the brooding, overall hush.

The earmarks of the dead animal, swallow fork left and underbit right, pretty much identified it as his own, but he wanted a look at the brand to make certain. So he ran a loop of rope on one leg of the critter, returned to his saddle, threw a dally, and set his tall buckskin to the pull. The carcass turned over, and the brand disclosed was a Bar 88, which made it certain.

He freed his rope, and while coiling it, kneed the buckskin here and there about the meadow, his glance on the earth. Presently, he found it — hoof sign, leading from this small stretch of benchland down through the timber toward the basin below. In the soft mat of forest duff, the sign was easy to follow, until presently the timber thinned and gave way to the long, open roll of the foothills. Here the sign was lost in a trampled tangle of deep-cut cattle trails that angled up and down, crossing and recrossing. Which did not matter particularly, as he had now worked out the general line of direction.

He hauled the buckskin to a stop, his glance swinging. Straightaway to the west across the wide basin miles, the Cold River Rim was a rugged scarp, dark and massive, frowning down upon the willow and alder-lined run of the river itself. Behind and above him, the Sentinel Range lifted in timbered loftiness, while directly below, where the sweep of the foothills sank into the basin floor, a brief smear of green marked a water seep.

Here also stood Price Tedrow's lath and tarpaper cabin, its windows giving off reflected glints of the westering sun. A shed of like flimsy construction and a small pole corral completed the barren, meager layout. In the corral a lone, ribby horse stood hip-shot, and an old, bow-topped wagon sagged beside the shed.

Held by his roughening thoughts, Howison made a still, rawboned, hard-muscled figure in his saddle, the harsh severity of his mood pulling his features into lean, angular lines. Pinched down and frowning, his eyes were a frosty gray against the deep-weather tan of his cheeks.

While he watched, a woman left the cabin, bucket in hand, trudging along to the boxed-in spring at the head of the water seep. Here she filled her bucket, then remained crouched beside the spring for a little time as though oppressed by a weariness of the spirit or of the flesh, or of both. When she did straighten and plod back to the cabin, shoulder sagging under the drag of her burden of water, it was with a dispirited slowness.

Deepening anger washed through Howison, toughening his purpose. Damn such people! Always so shiftless and forlorn. Ever on the narrow edge of want or need of some sort — even of outright hunger. So their condition nagged a man's conscience until he weakened and let them haul their ramshackle wagon up beside a water hole on his range. Whereupon they knocked together a rickety cabin and sat back waiting for the Lord to provide — along with an assist, of course, from a jelly-hearted mortal idiot by the name of Howison!

Yeah, that was how it was. You gave them a break, treated them fair and generous, and what thanks did you get? Why, they slow-elked one of your choice two year olds, hacked out a quarter and a loin, and left the rest to the green flies and the buzzards and the four-footed prowlers of the night that would slink in after dark and lift their coyote yodels to the stars.

Well, no time like the present to put a stop to that sort of miserable, treacherous business, once and for all! Howison sent the buckskin straight on downslope and over to the cabin.

The woman stepped out to face him. Once there might have been a real grace in her, along with a matching prettiness. But that would have been long ago, and over the hard, hard years she had left these precious possessions behind her. Now, under a shapeless calico dress she was gaunt and slightly stooped, her face lined with a resigned hopelessness, her hair a ragged, graying shroud falling loosely about her shoulders.

Facing her, meeting the whipped tragedy in her eyes, Howison's harsh resolve began to leak away. It dwindled still further when she made a toneless remark.

"The meat's in the shed. I haven't touched it. And I won't — not if I starve to death!"

"What meat?" asked Howison gruffly.

"You know — or you wouldn't be here."

He twisted in his saddle, looking past her, looking around. "Where's your husband, Mrs. Tedrow?"

"Town by this time, I expect. If they didn't lynch him before they got him that far. They threatened that they might!"

The words pulled Howison forward and leaning. "They! Who are they?"

She shrugged wearily, but in her eyes a show of spirit flared. "They had no right to take him, or threaten him like they did. Poor he might be, and shiftless at times — but Price Tedrow is no thief! So far as the world will allow, he's an honest man. I tell you he didn't do it. I don't care if they did find that meat hanging in our shed. Price Tedrow never put it there. Someone else did. Now — now . . ."

Moisture drowned out the flare of spirit in her eyes.

Uncomfortable before a woman's tears, Howison swung down and crossed to the shed, pushing open the sagging door. Strung to a low rafter with a piece of baling wire was the quarter and loin from the two year old lying dead back up there in the meadow in the timber. At the sight of it, anger partly lost now returned, and as

12

Howison went back to his horse, his face was stern, his eyes bleak.

Mrs. Tedrow had quieted again. She lifted her head with a sort of numbed dignity. "From one of yours?"

Howison nodded curtly. "From one of mine. You say your husband isn't responsible. If he isn't, who is?"

"I — I don't know. Price and me, we had no idea the meat was there. Early this morning we hitched the team to the wagon and went over to the river for some rocks to wall up the spring more securely. We'd hardly got back when they came riding in, talking loud how they were out to put a stop to the slow-elking and rustling that was going on if they had to hang every thieving nester in the country.

"My Price stood right up to them and told them he knew nothing about any rustling or slow-elking, which was the truth. They said they aimed to search the place, and Price told them to go ahead, as he had nothing to hide. Right off, they found the meat. After that — well . . ."

"They," probed Howison, "— who were they, Mrs. Tedrow? Strangers, or someone you knew?"

"Price called one of them by name. Labine, it was. That's it — Labine. So they put Price on one of our team and headed for town."

Howison stared off across a basin drenched with the afternoon's waning sunlight. Abruptly he brought his glance back to her. "This is the truth you've given me?"

She nodded with a swift vehemence. "I swear it! Even if Price was out to steal, it would never be from you, Mr. Howison. How could we possibly be that low, when you've treated us so kindly? Why we'd cut off our hands first. I'm not lying to you, Mr. Howison. I swear I'm not. You must believe me!"

He met the straining honesty in her eyes and spoke gruffly. "I do believe you."

He went into his saddle, started off, then hauled up the buckskin in mid-stride. "Don't let that meat go to waste, Mrs. Tedrow. It's yours, now — a gift from me. Use it. And I'll see that your husband gets safely back to you."

In a rush of gratitude, her newly regained composure began to break up again, so he reined quickly away, lifting the buckskin to a reaching lope.

Labine, he thought grimly. Jack Labine. And two others, Mrs. Tedrow had said. Two others who would have to be Nick

Bodie and Chirk Dennis. Sawbuck men, all of them. Which meant that behind them stood the heavy, thrusting figure of Ben Walrode . . .

It was a full eight miles from the Tedrow cabin to Basin City, so Howison soon pulled the buckskin down from a lope to a swinging jog, a distance gait. The sun, lowering toward the Cold River Rim, lost some of its earlier warmth, and a narrow belt of purple shadow began to build along the base of the rim. Though the many signs of late summer were still at hand, to one who knew this land well and understood the character of its days, there was the waiting breath of autumn hovering over it. In the loftier reaches of the Sentinels, aspen swamps were showing an ever-deepening stain of yellow-gold, while under the cold gray crags of Chancellor Peak, pockets of cherry brush were flushing with a first touch of their crimson fire.

Along the north-south run of the main basin road, a drift of dust spiraled up. Identifying the buckboard and team of sorrels scudding ahead of it, Howison cut over to intercept. And Henry Kleyburg hauled up his team and set the brake.

He was a man in his late fifties, grizzled about the temples, square-jawed and solid

15

in all his ways of living. With him were his womenfolk, wife and daughter. Howison lifted a saluting hand to his hat brim. "Good folks — Howdy!"

Mrs. Kleyburg smiled at him. "And how are you, David? Where have you been keeping yourself? It's been weeks since you last stopped by the ranch." She was a cheerful, motherly sort, warm-hearted and direct.

Before Howison could answer, Sue Kleyburg spoke.

"The man," she said pointedly, "has all the instincts of a hermit, besides being insufferably self-sufficient and his own best company. He should be living in a cave."

A glint of amusement pinched Howison's eye-corners. "Now — now, Susie! You do me wrong. I'm just a hard-working cowhand, trying to scratch out a living. You shouldn't hold that against me."

Sue Kleyburg flushed. She was a slim, pretty girl, still in her early twenties, but owning a maturity of poise and balance that made her seem older. She had her mother's deep-blue eyes and her father's quick and stubborn spirit, which her retort bore out.

"Smooth talk, Mister Howison. Too

smooth. And you'll have a real argument on your hands if you keep calling me Susie. The name, I'll have you understand, is Susan!"

Henry Kleyburg grumbled impatiently. "What kind of palaver is that? Dave, you're headed for town? Good! Means you'll eat supper with us at the Cottonwood." He looked down at his daughter with parental challenge. "You got any objections?"

Sue flushed again. "I suppose it can be endured."

"Bosh!" grunted her father. "Don't be so cussed contrary. You'll be there, Dave?"

Howison nodded. "Wouldn't miss it."

Kleyburg kicked off the brake, shook the reins, and the buckboard scudded away.

Howison held the buckskin back, letting the dust settle. His glance, following the Kleyburg rig, was narrowed and musing. The invitation to supper had been fair and friendly, but behind it lay a significance that he had not missed. He knew what Henry Kleyburg would probably ask him sometime during the meal. And he knew what his answer would be. It would not be the one Henry Kleyburg hoped for. This he regretted, as the Kleyburgs were the best of people, whom he admired and knew a real fondness for. Just the same, a man had to follow his own convictions. . . .

Town stood in the middle reaches of Jubilee Basin, in the angle formed by the confluence of Cold River with Big Stony Creek, which flowed in from the east off the flank of Chancellor Peak. The valley road passed through Basin City as its single street, then emerged to become the freight and stage route that crossed Big Stony by log bridge and followed the river south and west, down the narrow, swift-dropping confines of Horsehead Canyon to the outer world beyond.

Early twilight lay over the town, softening its outlines. The Kleyburg team and buckboard stood at the hitch rail of the Cottonwood Hotel, and Howison put the buckskin in beside it. As he stepped down, it was young Tap Geer who came sauntering, footloose and carefree. He showed Howison a quick, cheerful grin.

"Well, well, and well! Would you see who's with us. The big man from the head of Bannock Creek. Would he, I wonder, be just a mite thirsty?"

"Mister Geer, I believe," jibed Howison with mock disapproval. Then he smiled and slapped Tap on the shoulder. "How are you, boy?"

"Stone sober and reasonably honest," proclaimed Tap. "Though Ben Walrode might try and tell you different. What brings you to town, Dave? Don't tell me you've decided to join the ranks of the righteous, aiming to smoke out the devil and all his little helpers?"

Howison's smile deepened. "Understand there's to be a meeting of sorts along that line. Thought I might listen in."

"Just so listening is all you do," Tap warned. "Don't let Ben Walrode make a sucker of you."

"Hell with Ben Walrode!" Howison laid it out bluntly.

"Friend," approved Tap, "you speak my language. So I ask again — would you be a mite thirsty?"

"Presently," Howison promised. "First, I want a word with Milt Shannon."

Tap nodded. "I'll be waiting in the Ten Strike."

Sheriff Milt Shannon's office was in a lower front corner of the white-painted, two-storied courthouse. Shannon himself was a somewhat seedy-looking individual in whom considerable tenure in office had inspired caution rather than boldness. The politics of his position had become his major concern, and he played them to the hilt, acutely sensitive to every pulse beat of this Jubilee Basin range. When Dave Howison entered, Shannon was sitting at his desk, idly perusing a but lately arrived reward dodger in the uncertain light of a badly smoked up kerosene lamp. He leaned back, nodded a narrow head, and gave forth with what passed as a smile of welcome.

"Hello, Dave! Good to see you around for a change. Have a seat and explain yourself. How are things on Bannock Creek?"

"The usual," Howison returned briefly. He jerked a thumb toward the rear of the courthouse where stood the jail. "By chance, Milt, would you have anybody locked up?"

"By chance, I might." Shannon showed a shade of caution.

"Price Tedrow?"

"How'd you know?"

"Never mind. What's he in for?"

"Slow-elking."

"On whose say-so?"

Shannon stirred restlessly, a flicker of unease in his glance.

"Jack Labine brought him in. Jack and a couple of other Sawbuck boys. Made a citizen's arrest."

"Don't tell me!" Howison's sarcasm was deep and biting. "A citizen's arrest, eh?

Now that really is something! Because Jack Labine is one heck of an excuse of a citizen to be arresting anybody for anything. Talk about the man biting the dog!"

Some of Milt Shannon's meager amiability began to dry up.

"Labine's all right. He was just looking after the interests of Sawbuck and the other legitimate outfits in the basin. He and Bodie and Dennis caught Tedrow cold with the goods. Tedrow had the meat hung in his shed. He's lucky they brought him in instead of stringing him up on the spot. Which is something that's been known to happen to slow-elkers."

Howison's glance sliced bleakly across the murky light of the room, and his retort was harsh.

"Milt, that's a heck of a way for a man in your position to talk. I thought better of you. Or is it you've decided the protection of that star on your shirt doesn't reach as far as a nester's cabin?"

Slow color climbed through Shannon's cheeks. "You got no right to say that. What do you mean by it?"

"I mean you're being played for a fool. Those three so virtuous Sawbuck hands found slow-elked meat in Price Tedrow's shed, did they? How'd they know it was

21

slow-elked? Or didn't they bother to explain that part to you?"

"Well, no — they didn't," admitted Shannon reluctantly, his tone turning a little sulky. "Still and all, the meat was there. And where would a two-bit shanty nester get a whole loin and quarter of fresh beef if he didn't steal it?"

"For all you know, I may have given it to him. In any case, credit the man with enough common sense not to leave any stolen meat hanging around where the first nosey rider to come along would be sure to find it."

"A nester is dumb enough to do most anything," Shannon mumbled. "And I'll take the word of three honest cattle hands against that of a deadbeat nester any time. So unless Tedrow can come up with cast-iron proof that he didn't slow-elk the meat — well . . . !"

Howison got out tobacco and papers and twisted up a cigarette. As he lighted it, he looked across his cupped hands with rising anger and disgust.

"Milt, you know better than that. Price Tedrow doesn't have to prove he didn't do it. You got to prove that he did. That's the way the law reads, and that's the way I'm going to see that you read it. Did you, by chance, bother to ask Tedrow himself where the meat came from?"

"Now I sure as heck did. He said he didn't know where it came from. That somebody must have put it there while he and his woman were off hauling rocks or something. Who's going to believe that kind of lying talk?" Shannon showed a thin grimace that was more smirk than it was smile.

"This time," said Howison curtly, "it could be true. Don't bet your shirt that it isn't, else you could find yourself way out on a limb looking pretty silly to a lot of voters." He moved to the door. "Long as you have Tedrow locked up, you keep him so — and safe — until I leave town. Then I'll take him home with me."

Shannon jerked up in his chair, startled. "How do you figure that?"

He got no reply. Howison had already stepped out into the deepening twilight.

Milt Shannon settled slowly back in his chair, staring at the empty doorway, a little scowl of uncertainty furrowing his cheeks.

Outside, Howison stood for a time, looking up and down the darkening street. This, he thought, was one of the better hours to be in town. Day's heat was gone, and a small wind, sliding down from

Chancellor Peak, filtered across housetops and around corners, stirring the leaves of the three big cottonwood trees that stood in front of the hotel. On that cool, clean current rode the vital essences of space, along with the homey tang of fat pine-wood smoke from various supper chimneys. Sparrows chirped sleepily in the cottonwoods, and lamplight warmed windows and doorways. This was, mused Howison, the hour when man, down through all the ages, had crouched beside his home fire and found comfort and security there.

But what comfort or security for that lone woman with the tragic eyes, out at the Tedrow cabin?

Under the bite of this thought, he took a final drag at his cigarette and flipped the butt into the street's dust with a quick, disturbed gesture. After which, he angled over to the Ten Strike.

The place was comfortably filled. At the far end of the bar, Henry Kleyburg, Miles Sulivane, and old Jock Dunaway made a small group, trading range-land talk, with Sulivane holding forth on some point with a shrill emphasis. Over in the card-table area, Jack Labine, Chirk Dennis, and Nick Bodie were playing three-handed cutthroat. At the near end of the bar, Tap Geer stood

24

alone, a bottle and a pair of glasses in front of him. As Howison moved up beside him, Tap showed a twisted grin.

"Maybe, before mentioning this drink, Dave — I should have told you some people would say you're in bad company."

Howison studied his companion briefly. Knowing this young rider well, and liking him, he sensed a shade of tension behind the usual cheerful insouciance.

"Why should they?"

"Well," said Tap, moving his glass around in little circles on the bar, "it's like this. Ben Walrode has spread the word to keep an eye on Tap Geer. Because he's a bad, bad man. He was seen making talk with Jett Chesbro. That's Walrode's story."

"Any truth to it?" Howison asked. "I mean, you were seen with Chesbro?"

Tap nodded and went on to explain.

"Didn't mean a thing. I'd gone down along Horsehead Canyon after a deer for Barney Tuttle. The old boy likes his venison, but so stove up with his years he can't get out after some himself. A lot of times when I was light of pocket and between jobs, Barney fed me, so I figured it was my turn. I took a ride through Horsehead and knocked over a buck not more than fifty yards from the road.

25

"I gutted it and while it was cooling out, built a fire and cooked up some coffee. About then, Jett Chesbro came riding. Sure, I've heard talk of Jett being free and easy with other people's cows, but I never seen him working at it. He's never done me no harm, and I got nothing against him. So when he sniffed at the coffee, hungry-like, I told him to get down and have some.

"We talked bout this and that and nothin' in particular and had the pot near empty when the stage came by. Buck Pruitt, he saw us and waved his whip. Later, Jett helped me load the buck behind my saddle. Then he went his way, and I went mine. And that, so help me, is the all of it. But Buck Pruitt, he must have said something to somebody about seeing Jett with me, and it's got back to Walrode. Now the word is out to steer clear of Tap Geer. He's a bad one. He hangs out with cow thieves."

"Forget it," advised Howison. "Always some kind of talk goes on. While Jett Chesbro isn't exactly the sort maybe to pick for a bosom friend, at the same time it's none of Ben Walrode's business if you want to stake the man to a drink of coffee on casual meeting."

"That's how I figure it," said Tap.

"Speaking flat out, I don't give a darn what Ben Walrode thinks about me, but I sure don't like it when men like Henry Kleyburg and old Jock Dunaway and Miles Sulivane look at me slant-eyed and suspicious. Which they're doing right now."

"So I notice," Howison murmured. "Also, friend Labine has decided to move in. I wonder why?"

Jack Labine was high and lank, with a round head set close between pointed, bony shoulders. His features were rough, and his skin, dark burned by sun and weather, was grained and coarse, reflecting an oily shine under the yellow flare of the Ten Strike's hanging lamps. His eyes were small and so reddish brown in shade there seemed to be little currents of crimson stirring in them. He moved with a high-kneed stride as though each aggressive step emphasized his right, as riding boss of Ben Walrode's Sawbuck outfit, to go where he pleased and do as he pleased any time he pleased. It reflected an arrogance that Dave Howison had always found offensive, and he watched with no warmth when Labine squared away in front of Tap.

"Been hearing things about you, Geer," proclaimed the Sawbuck foreman. "Not good things, either. So here's a word of gospel for you to take to heart." The tone was gravelly, irritating. "Starting now, Big Stony Creek is a deadline for you. Don't let me catch you anywhere south of it. I do, then it's your neck. Understand?"

Whatever Tap Geer expected, it was nothing quite as blunt and unequivocal as this. For a moment, he was held in startled silence, unable to dredge up a suitable reply. However, quicker to react, Dave Howison now filled the interval with a biting sarcasm.

"Well, well, and well! Tap, have yourself a good look. We seem to have with us a sagebrush Caesar in leather pants!"

The crimson currents in Labine's eyes burned brighter.

"This is strictly none of your business, Howison. Keep out of it!"

"Not so," returned Howison. "It's always my business when a good man is told he can't ride across free land. When that happens, I take it upon myself to find out why? Suppose you tell me?"

Recovering to speak for himself, Tap did so with quick heat.

"I'll ride where I darn well please, Labine!"

"Not as a friend of Jett Chesbro, you won't." Labine turned to Howison again. "You wanted to know why? Well, now you do. Sawbuck range is closed territory to Chesbro and his crowd."

"Understandable," Howison admitted, ironically dry. "Only there are a couple of holes in your proposition, Labine. First, Sawbuck doesn't own all the range south of Big Stony — not by a heck of a lot. Ben Walrode would like to own it, of course. However, the point is, he doesn't. For the rest, Tap Geer is no part of Jett Chesbro's crowd, as you put it."

"I say he is," charged Labine. "He was seen sharing coffee with Chesbro."

Howison scoffed derisively. "Which means nothing. For instance, right now anybody in this room can see me talking to you. Does that mean we're close friends? What do you think?"

Being badgered and aware of it, Labine turned ugly.

"You should wake up, Howison. A lot of funny business is going on in this basin."

"Oh, I'm awake, all right," returned Howison caustically. "You got no idea how awake I am. And you're right about the funny business. Like you having the gall to slap a citizen's arrest on Price Tedrow for slow-elking. That's the funniest kind of business I know. What proof, for instance, did you have?"

"Bodie, Dennis, and me — we found the meat in Tedrow's shed."

Howison scoffed again. "Any man has the right to hang meat in his shed if he's a mind to."

"Not this kind." Labine's gravelly tone was rough and heavy. "Not meat off a slow-elked critter. Which this was. Heck, it hadn't even been skinned out; the hide was still on it."

"No, I noticed," Howison nodded. "It had been slow-elked, all right. And off a good two year old of mine. Only, Price Tedrow never butchered that animal. Someone else did. Would you, by chance, have any ideas along that line?"

Wariness filmed Labine's eyes. "I already named your man for you. Tedrow's the one."

"Not the way I read the sign," Howison told him coldly.

Labine shrugged his high shoulders and turned away. "You think what you think, I'll think what I think." He dropped a final word for Tap. "Remember, Geer — you've been told!"

Carrying in from the outer night, the mellow jangling of the iron triangle on the Cottonwood Hotel porch signaled the supper call. Immediately, the group at the far end of the bar broke up and moved to the door. As they passed, Henry Kleyburg's glance touched Howison.

"Remember, Dave — we're expecting you."

As the saloon door ceased winnowing, Tap Geer looked at Howison and spoke with a thin bitterness.

"You see, Dave? Something for you — something decent and friendly. But not even a nod for me."

Howison spun a coin across the bar to pay for the drinks and spoke softly.

"Stay tight in the saddle, boy. Go help Barney Tuttle eat some of that venison. I'll have something to say to Mister Ben Walrode, and then we'll see what we shall see! Just remember this. Any time you need help, you come to me. You know the trail to Bar 88."

Tap, brooding as they moved to the door, nodded.

"But it's a heck of a note when a man's treated like a sheep-killing coyote when he's done nothing to deserve it. I hope Ben Walrode chokes — him with his big mouth!"

CHAPTER

II

The dining room of the Cottonwood Hotel held one big center table and several smaller ones placed along the walls. At one of these the Kleyburg family sat, Henry Kleyburg and his wife on one side, daughter Sue on the other. There was also a fourth person at the table.

The sight of Ben Walrode seated beside Sue Kleyburg brought Dave Howison to momentary pause. All anticipation for the meal left him, and as he moved down the room, he took refuge behind an armor of reserve.

A vacant chair stood at the outer end of the table, and Henry Kleyburg waved him to it.

"Met up with Ben and invited him to sit in. Gives us a chance to maybe shape up a few ideas before the meeting tonight."

"Just so," agreed Ben Walrode heartily. "Things show some signs of getting out of hand here and there across the range, and it's up to responsible folks to do something about it."

Howison answered briefly as he took his chair. "Depends on where you stand to figure out what those things mean."

The curtness of the retort was not lost on Henry Kleyburg, who flashed Howison a quick, wondering glance.

"Sure, Dave," he soothed. "We all have our opinions. But on occasion we have to surrender them for the all-over good."

Howison shrugged. "Before I surrender any of mine, I want a good look at the cards — everybody's cards, and all of them!"

Walrode's show of heartiness shaded off somewhat. He was a big man, as tall as Howison, but weightier, with broad, fleshy cheeks. Smiling, his teeth showed big and square. In a darker mood, his mouth could turn heavy and sullen, even cruel. His hair was fair, his eyes pale, and now he was frowning.

"That carried a funny sound, Howison. Like you intended to stand way off by yourself. If we're to do a job of cleaning up this basin range, we got to get together in common cause."

"We can wait for the meeting to talk about that," Howison told him shortly.

"Just now I think Mrs. Kleyburg would prefer we talk of other things."

He was thanked by Mrs. Kleyburg's quick, gentle smile. "What's the gossip along Bannock Creek, David?"

Howison mused for a moment. "Nothing of real account. The days run one into another, and it seems Woody Biggs and me, we never quite manage to catch up with all the necessary chores. Woody claims the Lord figured things that way to keep men from growing lazy."

Mrs. Kleyburg laughed softly. "Woody Biggs — I haven't seen him in ages. Doesn't he ever leave the ranch any more?"

"Not if he can help it. Claims it a refuge from the wickedness of the world."

Mrs. Kleyburg laughed again. "That's Woody, all right — the old fraud! Always has a reason and an answer for everything."

Henry Kleyburg, direct and forceful in all things, liking to drive straight to the core of any objective, stirred in his chair, impatient to bring the conversation back to more serious matters. But now food arrived at the table, and the business of eating took over. Then Allie Langley, who ran the Cottonwood, came over to trade talk with Sue and her mother. So the meal was virtually done with before Kleyburg got his chance. When he did, he made quick use of it.

"Been thinking over that remark of yours, Dave. It troubles me. What's behind it?"

Howison's reserve deepened again. He shook his head. "Still better we leave it for the meeting, Henry."

Kleyburg gestured irritably. "We're all friends here."

"Now I should hope so," put in Walrode. He went on smoothly. "Anyone would think, Howison, that you have something on your mind you're afraid to let go of."

"I'll let go of it," Howison promised curtly, "at the proper time and place. Which isn't here. As a guest at this table, I'm trying to act like one by avoiding arguments."

The retort was barbed and color-stained Ben Walrode's broad cheeks. Serenely wise and alert to all the signs, Mrs. Kleyburg pushed back her chair. "You men scatter along and have your old meeting. David is right, here is no place to argue out your differences."

Henry Kleyburg and Ben Walrode were up immediately, Kleyburg looking at his wife. "Don't know how long this will take. If it gets late, maybe you better arrange with Allie Langley to put us up for the night."

Mrs. Kleyburg shook her head. "Even if it's way past midnight, we're going home. I like to watch the dawn come up through my own kitchen window."

The cowman grunted and turned away, Walrode with him. Howison moved to follow, but Mrs. Kleyburg restrained him softly.

"A moment, David — please!"

He eased back, his glance wondering. She was thoughtful, the shadow of some concern darkening her eyes.

"You know Henry pretty well, David — how impulsive and sometimes heedless he can be in his judgments. Have you any idea what he has in mind now?"

"I think so," nodded Howison. "But it is my feeling that it is something which originated with Ben Walrode."

"It is," Mrs. Kleyburg said with swift feeling. "It is — exactly that. And I don't want my husband assuming responsibilities — and liabilities — that are not rightfully his in the first place. If Ben Walrode wants to set up some kind of cattleman's protective association here in Jubilee Basin, let him head it himself instead of trying to talk my Henry into the spot."

Sue Kleyburg, silent and — so Howison thought — rather subdued during the meal, now spoke up.

"Mother, I think you're making a great deal out of nothing. Ben isn't trying to talk Dad into anything. Besides, Dad's no child. He knows what he's doing."

"I'm not so sure of that," returned Mrs. Kleyburg gravely. "I haven't lived thirty years with Henry Kleyburg without coming to know him pretty well, better than anyone else. Even better at times, I've found, than he knows himself. Your father, my dear, has a streak of crusader spirit in him, and when he gets started on what he feels is a worthwhile cause, he doesn't always pause to consider the possible consequences. While I do. So I say again, if Ben Walrode believes his idea such a great one, let him march at the head of it himself."

Sue started to frame a reply, instead turned to Howison. "Mother shows she can be pretty set in her ideas, too. What's your opinion?"

"I think," he told her carefully, "that your mother is a very wise person. And that you should heed what she says."

Sue made a face at him. "Oh, you . . . ! You're just as bad as she is. You make it sound like something was being put over on Dad. Like you didn't trust Ben."

"That," said Howison evenly, "is correct. I don't!"

Sue stiffened. "Indeed! And why not?"

He tipped a shoulder. "Afraid you wouldn't believe me if I told you."

She studied him gravely. "You don't like Ben, do you, Dave? You never have. What have you got against him?"

"Just that he is — Ben Walrode. And maybe," Howison added, gently dry, "because he's too good a friend of yours."

Sue flushed. "That's ridiculous," she charged tartly. "To dislike anyone for no better reasons than those."

"Just the same, in this case, that is how it is with me." Howison was still gentle about it. He stood up. "Mother Kleyburg, I'll say what I think you'd like me to say at the meeting. It may help."

"I hope so," sighed Mrs. Kleyburg fervently. "And thank you, David."

Sue Kleyburg was still combative. "Right now I'm more than half mad at both of you. Ben Walrode's all right. And I don't think you should hint that he isn't."

Howison grinned at her tightly. "Not only hinting, Susie — but saying it! And repeating the fact that your mother is very, very wise."

He left it so, pausing in the hotel entrance to build an after-supper cigarette. But he had left his grin with Sue Kleyburg. Now, as he stepped into the night's full dark and went along the street to Milt Shannon's office, there was the taut pull of decision about his lips.

The office was more brightly lighted than it had been earlier in the evening. The murmur of men's voices came as Howison neared the open doorway. He paused there, his glance marking those present. It was about as he thought it would be. Besides Henry Kleyburg and Ben Walrode, there were Miles Sulivane and Jock Dunaway holding down chairs. Against the far wall, Pete Mallory squatted on his heels and sucked at a black and battered pipe. Mallory ran a one-man spread in the lavas over past the Cold River Rim. He was an independent soul, and he showed Howison a cheerful nod.

Sheriff Milt Shannon sat behind his desk. He had cleaned and trimmed the lamp, and in its stronger glow his expression showed a strict and guarded neutrality.

With Howison's arrival, Henry Kleyburg spoke with his usual impatient drive.

"Looks like everybody who counts is on hand, so we might as well get started.

We've a fair idea of why we're here. But just to be sure, maybe Ben should go over the trail again."

Walrode cleared his throat, his glance roving to gauge the impact of his words.

"It's like this. Some of us are losing cattle. Not a great many just now, perhaps. But it can become serious if allowed to go on. Like any other kind of thief, the more booty a cattle rustler can get away with, the more he'll go after. So the time to stop him is before he gets too big and too bold.

"Henry and I have talked the matter over and feel that perhaps we solid cattlemen should get together in a protective organization of some sort that could act in the common interest of all of us. What do you think? Let's have some opinions."

He said it smoothly and easily, a big, convincing figure with the smoke of his cigar curling past his broad features.

"I'm all for it, of course," approved Henry Kleyburg immediately. "Why just the word of such an organization would discourage some of the thieves, active or would-be. And any others who need to be convinced that we mean business can find it out on the end of a rope, if necessary."

"Right — right!" chimed Miles Sulivane thinly. "That's the talk for me. I'm not after raisin' beef to fill the belly of any rustler. Nor yet his pockets!"

Sulivane was a waspy, acid little Irishman, bent and gnarled from a lifetime of hardship and toil, and made penurious by it. An honest man, but one who could turn as savage and vindictive as a wolf in defense of what he felt to be his lawful rights.

Old Jock Dunaway was a mild man and one whose advanced years made any kind of support from others attractive, and he now nodded his slow agreement, his Scotch brogue a rolling burr.

"I'll go along. For-r 'tis good sense."

Ben Walrode looked at Mallory. "Pete?"

Mallory grinned. "I'm kinda just listenin' in on this business. Besides, I ain't big enough to amount to a darn, either way."

"There you're wrong," Walrode countered. "You're more than big enough to add one more good man on our side."

Mallory was still wary. "Sorta used to ridin' my own trail, and like it that way. Know just where I stand, then. No matter what comes up, I got nobody to blame but myself. By the way — who's set to ramrod this here organization? I mean, who'll be the herd bull? You, Walrode?"

"I'd like to see Henry Kleyburg take over," Walrode said. "I see him as the logical man for the job, being the most influential cattleman in the basin. His opinions and what he stands for will carry a lot of weight. Suit you, Pete?"

"I'm still listenin'," evaded Mallory briefly.

Swinging his heavy shoulders with a show of irritation, Ben Walrode came around to face Dave Howison.

"What's it with you, Howison? Changed your mind since supper? Or aren't there enough cards on the table? As I recall, you wanted to look at a lot of them."

Here was an edge of challenge, but for the moment Howison let it pass, giving no direct answer. Instead, he put his glance on Milt Shannon.

"Let's hear what our worthy sheriff thinks about it. He's the law in these parts. How about it, Milt? You ready to turn the authority of your office over to a gang of long-riding, self-righteous cowhands?"

Shannon squirmed, looking up at him in grumbling resentment. "That's no kind of question to throw at me. Puts me right out in the middle of the street. You know darned well that no matter which way I turn there'll be some who won't like it."

"Sure, Milt — I know," agreed Howison sardonically. "But that's how it is with a job like yours. Bound to come a time when you have to start working at it. So, how about it? Do you or don't you police this range?"

"Hold on a minute, Dave!" Henry Kleyburg broke in and was stern about it. "Don't try and herd Milt into a corner. He's not about to let go of any of his authority, but he will get help from us. This is a big range, and one man can't be everywhere at all times. So why shouldn't we organize together to help him? What's wrong with that? Finally — and speaking personally — I don't care to be classed as a long-riding, self-righteous cowhand. Coming from you — I don't take that kindly."

"Wasn't referring to you, Henry," Howison told him quietly.

Ben Walrode did not miss the opening. "In that case, just who were you referring to?"

Here again was the challenge, and this time Howison met it head on. "All right, Ben, let's take the gloves off. Let's lay some facts on the line, get them right out in the open where everybody can get a good look at them. And, Henry, you'll be wise to listen close and do some solid thinking. Before you get wangled into a spot that could do you no good."

Still disgruntled, Kleyburg waved an impatient hand and gave short retort. "You got anything to say that's so darned important, get it off your chest."

"Fair enough," Howison said steadily. "See what you think of this. On my way to town I saw a flock of buzzards circling up in the Sentinels. I swung by that way and found a two year old of mine that had been slow-elked. There was horse sign leading down toward Price Tedrow's cabin, and I went down there. A loin and a quarter of that two year old was hanging in Tedrow's shed."

"Just some of what Henry and Ben been talkin' about," shrilled Miles Sulivane. "Slow-elkin's rustling, ain't it? Darn nester should be hung!"

"Not so fast, Miles," cautioned Howison. "You're jumping at conclusions. Tedrow didn't butcher that beef, and he didn't hang the meat in his shed, either. Somebody else did."

Sulivane blinked. "How do you figure that? You say the meat was slow-elked and you found it in Tedrow's shed. What more do you want?"

"The truth, Miles. And when I get it, I'll

take care of the rest myself. I'll stomp my own snakes, not ask someone else to do it for me. That is, unless Milt Shannon takes over as he should."

Henry Kleyburg was really disturbed now. "What's the rest of it?" he growled. "Got to be more than what you've given us."

"There is," Howison said. "Three of those long-riding cowhands I spoke of showed at Tedrow's place earlier and saw that meat, too. I'm wondering how they happened to be there in the first place, nosing around a nester cabin that's well inside my range. Wondering, too, why they should claim they were looking for slow-elked meat. And how it happened they knew exactly where to look for it. Strange business, I call it. In fact, too strange for me to swallow whole. What do you think, Henry?"

Kleyburg frowned. "I'm like Miles, here. You found a slow-elked animal and then found the meat in Tedrow's shed. That strikes me as pretty conclusive evidence. Yet you'd say Tedrow had nothing to do with it. What proof you got that he didn't?"

"Common sense. Plus a good woman's word."

Kleyburg waved that impatient hand of his. "Go on — go on! What woman? And where does the common sense come in?"

"For the first — Mrs. Tedrow. For the second, Tedrow himself would never be fool enough to hang slow-elked meat where the first person to come along would be sure to find it. The man's no complete idiot."

"He's a nester, which is good enough for me," put in Miles Sulivane. "I never saw one of such who ever told the truth or who wouldn't steal anything he could lay hands on. That goes for his woman, too."

Howison came around on him curtly.

"Easy, Miles! Keep that mean tongue of yours off Mrs. Tedrow. She's a good woman and an honest one. When she looked me in the eye and told me her husband had nothing to do with that shady business, I knew I was listening to the truth."

Feisty and contentious, Sulivane began to bristle, but Kleyburg headed him off. "Take it slow, everybody! We're here to consider something based on mutual trust and friendship, not wrangle all night. Dave, what three riders found that meat?"

"Jack Labine, Nick Bodie, and Chirk Dennis."

"My men, all," admitted Ben Walrode

quickly. "And reliable. If they say they found the meat in Tedrow's shed, that's where it was."

"Sure it was," Howison agreed with open irony. "I saw it there myself. But what interests me is — who put it there? And why?"

Ben Walrode had been chewing on a half-smoked cigar that had gone cold and sour. He examined it with a gesture not entirely gentle, then threw it into the battered brass spittoon at the end of Milt Shannon's desk.

"Seems to me, Howison, that you're reaching a long way for something that isn't there. I wouldn't know what it would be and I doubt you really do, either. So it would seem we're wasting time over nothing."

To this, Henry Kleyburg nodded troubled agreement. "Let's get on with our business."

"Presently, Henry," countered Howison. "I'm not through yet."

"That's it, Dave," encouraged Pete Mallory, half jocular, half serious. "Stay with 'em! Me, I'm interested in this little go-round. What did Price Tedrow himself have to say about it?"

"Haven't had a chance to talk to him," Howison said dryly. "You see, Pete —

Labine and company took it upon themselves to haul Tedrow to town on a citizen's arrest, and friend Milt here has him locked up."

Pete Mallory pushed his shoulders against the wall and came erect, exclaiming:

"Citizen's arrest! That's what you meant by long-riding, high and mighty cowhands. Well now, that particular breed of citizen better never try anything of the sort on me. They do, they get dusted up with a Winchester. What right they got, anyhow, nosin' around other folks's property?"

Howison smiled tightly. "Maybe we should let Ben answer that one, Pete."

Walrode flared, a show of heat in his cheeks, his pale glance hardening.

"My men act under my orders. Like Miles, I'm not raising beef to fill the pockets or bellies of any rustler, big or little. When I start losing cattle — and I have, some — then I'll put a stop to it if I have to search every nester shanty in Jubilee Basin, and take a look under every saddle fender that could be hiding a running iron. Like it or not, Howison, that's the way it's going to be."

"Right!" approved Miles Sulivane vigorously. "I'm with you, Ben."

Howison shrugged. "You sound real

noble, Ben. While you're at it, you better slow down your man Labine. He may figure he's nine feet high, but I don't see him so. The same goes for you. You own some range south of Big Stony Creek, but you don't own it all."

Walrode stared. "Now what are you driving at? I never claimed to own it all. What gave you that crazy idea?"

"Something your man Labine said. He set up a deadline against a friend of mine. He told Tap Geer it would be his neck if he ever again got caught riding south of Big Stony."

Walrode laughed curtly. "Oh, that! What's wrong with it? Where Sawbuck is concerned, Big Stony will always stand as a deadline against any and all cattle thieves. In particular that applies to Jett Chesbro and any of his crowd. If your good friend Geer doesn't want to be suspect, he should be more careful of the company he keeps."

"Right!" ranted Sulivane again. "I understand Geer was seen playing real cozy with Chesbro."

Mindful of the promise he had made Mrs. Kleyburg, Howison now looked at her husband. "There you see it, Henry. The sort of thing you're about to get mixed up in. Everybody — innocent or guilty — to be judged and pushed around as Ben Walrode happens to feel at the moment. So, before getting into Ben's grand scheme any deeper, I suggest you think it over, long and careful."

Marking the cattleman's expression, Howison saw that his words were wasted, were in fact, resented. Growling, Kleyburg gave another of his impatient, irritated gestures.

"Capable of making my own judgments."

Ben Walrode laughed. "There you have it, Howison. Henry feels he's quite old enough to think for himself. Also, he hasn't any more use for a cow thief, or for Jett Chesbro and his crowd, than I have. Neither has Miles here, or Jock. Or are they afraid to face up to the issue? You, apparently, are."

All afternoon and evening, from the moment of finding his slaughtered beef animal up in the Sentinels, a tide of slow anger had been building up in Dave Howison. Up to now he had kept it fairly in check. But here it came flooding up, taut and bitter, and it got away from him.

"That," he said bleakly, "was the card I waited to see, Ben. Now you listen close. Anybody who names Tap Geer a cow thief, or one of Jett Chesbro's crowd, is a liar! If the boot's your size, Ben, put it on. And if Tap Geer wants to ride south of Big Stony, he can do so any time he wants. To make that stick, if necessary, I'll ride with him. And let's see you, or any of your bully boys, stop us. If you want to argue the point right down to the wire, why now's as good a time as any. Go ahead and open the show if you feel that way!"

The words fell ominously, their meaning unmistakable. They held every man in the room taut and still. It was as though a chill wind had rushed through, touching all with a biting breath. High color congested Walrode's cheeks, and his mouth became heavy and ugly.

Henry Kleyburg was the first to recover. He dropped a hand on Howison's arm, his growl worried and placating. "That's no way to talk, Dave. Do me a favor. Get out of here. Go on home. Then come by the ranch tomorrow and talk things out with me."

Held with that sudden reckless anger, Howison knew a hostile moment even with this man he liked and respected so. But the concern in Kleyburg's eyes was very real, so he relented, nodding.

"All right, Henry — as a favor to you." He turned to Milt Shannon. "I'm taking

Price Tedrow home with me, Milt. Go get him!"

Shannon hesitated briefly, then got up and went out. He was soon back with the nester, who blinked around uncertainly before squaring a pair of thin shoulders and speaking with a tight stubbornness.

"No matter what any of you do or say, you can't make me admit to something I never did. I didn't slow-elk nobody's beef critter or hang any meat in my shed."

"Of course you didn't," Howison assured him. "I know that. So I'm taking you home."

Standing, Milt Shannon had blocked off the light of his desk lamp. Now, as he resumed his chair, the freed radiance spread, and Howison, stepping closer to Tedrow, exclaimed, "Man — you've been worked over! Who did it?"

At his best, Price Tedrow would always be an insignificant figure, just now more so than usual. His narrow face, smudged with a draggle of beard, was stained with bruises. His lips were puffed and split, and one eye, circled with dark discoloration, was swollen nearly shut. Smears of dried blood bracketed his mouth and chin, and more of the same spattered the front of his calico shirt.

To Howison's startled query, the nester hesitated. Howison reassured him. "You're in the clear. You got nothing to be afraid of. Who did it?"

"Them fellers who got hold of me did," mumbled Tedrow. "That Labine and the other two. All the way to town they kept tryin' to make me say I'd been slow-elking, and when I wouldn't, because I didn't, they got pretty mean. Finally, Labine he told that Bodie feller to use his fists on me, and Bodie did. Hauled me off my horse and cuffed me around some."

For a little time, Howison stood silent, just looking at Milt Shannon. Fully aware of what was in Howison's mind, Shannon would not meet his glance.

"Milt," said Howison with scathing contempt, "I'm afraid you're turning out pretty poor stuff. Maybe you should be retired!"

He turned then and led Price Tedrow out into the night.

Pete Mallory likewise moved to the door, pausing there for a last word and making no attempt to hide his feelings.

"All of a sudden," he drawled cuttingly, "I can't stand the smell of this room!"

Then he, too, stepped into the outer dark.

CHAPTER

III

Sifting down off Chancellor Peak, the night wind carried a deepening chill, and as they stood in the street's gloom, Dave Howison realized that the man beside him was shivering.

"Easy, Tedrow," he soothed. "I tell you there's nothing to fear now."

"Ain't what you think," explained the nester apologetically. "I ain't scared of nothin'. But that jail is a regular freeze box, and I ain't warmed up yet."

Howison immediately steered him toward the Ten Strike. "You need a couple of whiskeys."

"Hope Cass Garvey'll throw in some free lunch," Tedrow said. "I ain't had nothin' since early breakfast."

"You mean," Howison rapped, "that Milt Shannon locked you up and didn't feed you?"

"Nary a bite. Mebbe he forgot. Or figured a feller like me didn't rate any grub."

Howison had no answer to this, but the cold anger he had raised in Shannon's office surged anew. He pushed through the door of the Ten Strike and rang a coin on the bar.

"Whiskey for my friend here, Cass. And some free lunch to go with it."

It was harsh demand, rather than request. Behind the bar, Cass Garvey shrugged lumpy shoulders and set out bottle and glass.

"Plenty of both and what they're here for. Help yourself."

Price Tedrow poured, his hand shaking so that the neck of the whiskey bottle chimed faintly against the rim of the glass. He downed the drink at a gulp, squinting his eyes and tightening his lips against the fiery jolt of the liquor. He sighed deeply and looked at Howison.

"I sure needed that. Mighty decent of you, Mr. Howison. Hope I can favor you someday."

"Forget it," said Howison. "Tamp that one down with another, then get some food into yourself."

In the card-table area, Jack Labine and his two cronies were still at their game and arguing idly over it. But now the argument dried up and they sat staring. Then Labine pushed out of his chair and came stamping over to the bar, where he drove an elbow into Price Tedrow's shrinking ribs.

"What's the idea, Howison? This fellow should be in jail. How did he get out?"

"Through the door," returned Howison curtly. "I had Milt Shannon turn him loose. Any objections?"

"Plenty! He's a slow-elker."

"And you're a liar!" The words were as chill as Howison's glance. "I just gave Ben Walrode the lie on the same account. He took it. How about you?"

Cass Garvey, busy polishing a glass, set it carefully down and shifted aside a couple of strides. He spread both hands palm down on the bar top and stood so, still and watchful. At the same time, the door of the saloon swung open, letting in Pete Mallory.

Both moves were mere flickers at the edge of Howison's awareness, for the core of his attention was strictly on Labine. The words he had laid out so flatly were fighting ones, as he had intended they be. Now, poised and ready, he awaited Labine's reaction.

The Sawbuck foreman squared around, lips pulling slightly from his teeth. It was, Howison thought, akin to the first lip lift of a mean and snarling dog. But though the crimson fires in Labine's eyes were flaring, there was, also, far back in them, a measure of caution, as though Labine, finding himself faced suddenly with something he had neither expected nor guessed at, had turned wary.

Over at the card table, Nick Bodie, thick-set and burly, started to his feet, but dropped back as Pete Mallory's meaning drawl reached him.

"Stay put, Bodie! And you, Dennis. This is between Dave Howison and Labine. Leave it so!"

Price Tedrow spoke up anxiously. "No need gettin' in a row on my account, Mr. Howison. I don't mind what they call me, so long as they leave me alone to mind my own business."

"That's just the big trouble," Howison told him. "They didn't leave you alone, and they won't. Not if allowed to get away with it. This Sawbuck outfit seems set to mind everybody's business but their own, and some of us don't cotton to that idea. How about it, Labine, you got anything more to say?"

Jack Labine was tough and had faced more than one showdown in his life, both with fists and guns. When conditions warranted it and the time and setup was right, he was not afraid to face another. But he knew it was never smart to stand up to the call of someone as cocked and primed as Dave Howison was at this moment. Not unless the issue was important enough to justify the gamble. In his judgment, it was not so now. He shrugged and turned away.

"If Milt Shannon let him loose, I guess that's it. But Howison, one of these days — if you're still so proud and looking for a party — you'll be obliged, don't worry. Yeah, you'll be obliged!" He looked over at Bodie and Dennis. "All right, boys. Time to ride."

As they started for the door, Pete Mallory hauled up in front of them, speaking curtly.

"Just a minute, Labine. I've heard about a couple of things I don't like. One is a deadline you figure to set up along Big Stony. The other is this business of snoopin' around where you got no business and actin' like you were the law, the court, and God Almighty Himself. You try either of them deals on me, you'll find yourself on the wrong end of a Winchester. That's it!"

Jack Labine gave no answer other than a searing glance as he pushed by and went out, Bodie and Dennis at his heels. Howison watched them go. As the door quit winnowing, he turned back to the bar.

"Pour a couple, Cass. I've a taste in my mouth I want to wash out. Pete, how about you?"

Pete Mallory moved in beside him. "You know, Dave, this could be my last chance to drink friendly-like with anybody for a long time. Because I'm one of the little fellers, and as I see it, all my kind are in for one heck of a spell of misery. What I just told Labine, I sure meant. I'm a peaceful man if I'm left alone, but I'll throw a gun if I have to."

Cass Garvey, pouring, spoke with slow care. "This one is on the house. Being in business, I can't be yes and I can't be no. Not openly. But," he added, wagging his head soberly, "I got to admit I liked things the way they used to be. Everybody friends. Nobody out to push somebody else around."

It was just short of midnight when Dave Howison and Price Tedrow rode up to the latter's cabin. All the way from town Howison's big buckskin had fretted the bit, heading home and knowing it, and impatient for its own corral. But he had held it down to the plodding gait of Tedrow's wagon horse.

Lamp glow outlined the cabin window.

"Lettie's waitin' up," Tedrow decided. "Likely some worried on my account. Them fellers, Labine and the others, they made some scary talk in front of her before haulin' me off to town. She'll be wantin' to thank you, Mr. Howison, for treatin' me so fair."

"No need of thanks," Howison said. "You got a gun around the place?"

"An old .44 Winchester. Still shoots good, though. Why?"

"Should Labine or any of the rest of that crowd come bothering again, break it out and use it."

"Don't know as I'd be up to that," Tedrow said hesitantly. "I ain't never shot at any human. I don't like the idea of it."

"Naturally. But any man has the right to defend his home and his family."

"Oh, I'd do that, right enough," Tedrow decided. "Where Lettie is concerned, I mean. I'd shoot any man who ever laid a wrong hand or word on her."

The cabin door opened and against the light stood the gaunt figure of Tedrow's wife. Her call came anxiously across the dark.

"That you, Price?"

"Yeah, Lettie, it's me."

"You all right?"

"All right. Mr. Howison saw I got home safe."

"You thank him," the woman called. "You thank him a lot. He's been mighty good to us."

Howison reined the buckskin away and from a quick distance looked back to see Price Tedrow move into that humble doorway and the thankful arms of the wife who had waited out the anxious hours. Some of the night's lingering bitterness left him. If such were needed, he decided, this was thanks enough. . . .

Given its head, the buckskin really lined out for home, and Howison let it go. On either hand, the dark land flowed by and the breath of it, vital with its wild scents and flavors, was a chill tide against his face. On his right, the Sentinels towered black against the stars and off to the left in the flat heart of the basin, stirred by the rush of the buckskin's passing, a cow bawled, lifting a single lonely note across the night's far emptiness.

On this familiar trail, the buckskin reached Bannock Creek at the lower ford, splashed across and swung right, breasting the lift of the low slope. Ahead, a glint of light told of someone still awake at the home ranch, too.

Breaking from its faster gait to a slowing trot, the buckskin eased in beside the corrals, gave a long, panting breath of satisfaction, then shook itself until Howison's saddle gear creaked and rattled. Moving up out of the gloom, Woody Biggs spoke words of mild reproof.

"Must have been quite a meetin' to keep you up this late. Or was it a poker game in Cass Garvey's place, with you losin' your shirt?"

Darkness hid Howison's small grin. Woody Biggs was old enough to be his father, and at times, when he felt it justified, assumed an attitude close to being just that.

"No poker," Howison told him. "Just a clutter of other things. How come you're night-hawking, instead of in your blankets?"

"Your fault," retorted Woody crustily. "What with you bein' a mite slow to catch fire, but plenty brash when you do get stirred up, I got to frettin' some. Because it's in my bones that one of these days you and Ben Walrode are due to tangle, and when you do, I aim to be on hand."

They cared for the buckskin, then crossed to the ranch house where a fire was still alive in the kitchen stove and a pot of coffee steamed gently. Woody poured for both of them, then backed up to the stove's warmth, his cup cradled in both hands. He was a long, gaunt old man, grizzled and leathery. From under frosty, frowning brows he peered at Howison, who had slacked down in a chair.

"All right," prodded the old fellow. "You said there was a clutter of other things. What about 'em? Let's have it."

Howison gave out the essential facts of the afternoon and evening. Woody Biggs shook a worried head.

"Ben Walrode has his way, he'll tear this basin wide open. I can't figure Henry Kleyburg not realizin' that."

"Henry's a good man," Howison defended. "But like all of us, he has a blind spot or two. With him, Ben Walrode is one of them. I'll be talking with Henry again, tomorrow."

Woody scowled over another thought. "The two year old you found — it was one of ours?"

Howison nodded. "Ours."

"And you say that nester, Tedrow, didn't do it. If he didn't, who did?"

Howison drained his cup, got to his feet, yawning and stretching. "I'll try to explain that to Henry Kleyburg tomorrow."

"Heck with Kleyburg!" grumbled Woody. "Explain it to me."

Howison's grin showed again. "If I have to, then you're not as wise as I figured you were."

Woody grunted. "I could make a couple of guesses and not be too far wrong, I bet."

"I bet you could, too," Howison agreed. Once more he yawned and stretched. "Been a long day."

Along with her other charms, Sue Kleyburg possessed a luxurious head of auburn hair, which was at once her glory and her cross. A cross when she had to labor with its heavy folds while washing it, but a glory when she had finished and it became soft and gleaming in the morning sun. It was that way now as she sat on the steps of the Kleyburg ranch house, brushing it.

She wielded the brush somewhat mechanically, her thoughts elsewhere and vastly troubled. The ride home from town, late last night, had been anything but a pleasant one. Her father had been gruff and uncommunicative when she and her mother inquired about the results of the cattlemen's meeting. They got little from him that was definite, and what they did manage to dredge up was unsettling and the main cause for Sue's present depressed mood.

There had been, so her father reluctantly admitted, an open break between Dave Howison and Ben Walrode, something far more serious than just an ordinary difference of opinion. Dave Howison, so her father said, had expressed open hostility toward Walrode, even to the extent of challenging him to the ultimate showdown.

This had upset Sue badly. It had kept her awake long after she got to bed and was with her first thing when she awoke this morning, troubled and subdued. For these two, Dave Howison and Ben Walrode, were men she had long known and been friendly with, who had visited her in her home and in turn had squired her to Jubilee Basin's occasional social affairs. She had long been aware of a friction between them, a basic antagonism that, while distressing her to some extent, had never seemed serious enough to lead to open conflict — at least not such serious conflict. But now it had, and the fact frightened and depressed her.

She had tried to shake clear of this dark mood by getting her mind on something else, even to the chore of washing her hair. But that had done little good, either, for her gloom persisted, leaving her wan and weary.

In a dress of blue and white checked gingham, and her hair a burnished, shimmering cape across her shoulders, she looked younger and more girlish than usual to Dave Howison as he rode up and tied the buckskin to the iron ring stapled to the trunk of the cottonwood tree at the corner of the ranch house. He moved over to where she sat, dropped down beside her, and made an admiring observation.

"You know, Susie — when you want to work at it, you sure do a job of prettying up the world. You're a bright light in a weary universe."

She flushed slightly, and her glance struck slanting and defiant.

"I don't feel so," she told him curtly. "What brings you riding so early in the day?"

"Your pa wants to give me a talking to. Where is he?"

"Out around the corrals somewhere, doctoring a wire-cut horse. From what he told Mother and me on our way home last night, you've a talking to coming. Also, a good beating, for that matter."

Howison grinned and touched a shining tress. "Just like spun gold. Now if your disposition was as shiny, you'd be my sweet Susie of old."

A toss of her head switched her hair over her far shoulder.

"Never mind my disposition. You're the troublemaker, not me."

Howison assumed a distant expression. "Susie, you need a cure for the blues. You need a nice long ride through the right kind of country with the right person. The right country is the high reaches of the Sentinels, and the right person is me. How about it? Hop into your riding togs and we'll make a day of it. This is the best time of the year in the high country. The aspens and the cherry brush are coloring, and the deer are fat and frisky. Mighty pretty country up there. Most folks don't get a close look at it often enough. Do we go?"

"I think it's a splendid idea." It was Mrs. Kleyburg who spoke from the doorway behind them. "I'll put up a lunch for you. And if I were ten years younger, I'd make that ride myself. Good morning, David!"

"Morning, ma'am!" Howison came to his feet. To Sue he added, "You see? Like I told you last night, your mother is very, very wise."

Sue sputtered. "I know — you two . . . ! Whenever you get together . . ."

"Swell!" enthused Howison quickly. "Then it's all settled. While you change, I'll go take my scolding from your pa." Before she could think up a refusal, he was striding off, dropping a final caution over his shoulder. "Best bring along a coat of some sort; it gets pretty crisp up around Chancellor Peak."

Sue turned to her mother in exasperation. "I didn't say I'd go with him — or that I wanted to. I don't care to be shanghaied!"

"Which you are not," her mother returned calmly. "You're just being advised. Moping around here isn't doing you or anyone else any good. Go along and enjoy yourself."

"But after what Dad told us last night — how Dave acted — and the things he said . . ."

"It happens," stated Mrs. Kleyburg firmly, "that David Howison and I pretty much agree on certain issues and certain people. If our opinions happen to differ from that of your father, well — did it ever strike you that we could be right and your father wrong? Understand me — Henry Kleyburg is a fine man. No one appreciates that fact more than I do. But he is mortal and far from being infallible in his judgments. So, be sensible. Go change. It will do you good."

Howison met Henry Kleyburg crossing from the corrals to the saddle shed. The cattleman carried a can of axle grease in one hand and a bottle of balsam oil in the other. He deposited these two items inside the shed door and turned to Howison, wiping his hands on a piece of burlap sacking.

"Gelding in the saddle string tangled with a chunk of wire in the back pasture," he explained gruffly. "Been a mule, it would have stood quiet until somebody came along to work it clear without it getting scarred up. But the fool horse had to spook and fight the wire, so it lost some chunks of hide. A mule would have shown better sense."

"Just so," Howison agreed. "Henry, I've asked your daughter to go riding with me. All right with you?"

Kleyburg grunted. "Why shouldn't it be? She's gone riding with you before without having to ask my permission. Why ask it now?"

"You seemed kind of wound up at me last night."

"Still am, where last night is concerned. But what's that got to do with Sue riding with you?"

Howison tipped a shoulder. "Thought it might," he said dryly. "Figured it best to make sure."

Kleyburg searched his pockets for a pipe, packed it with rough cut, scratched a sulphur match against the shed door, and studied Howison levelly while puffing the pipe to a glow.

"That was strong talk you made to Ben Walrode," he growled finally. "You didn't mean all of it, of course?"

Howison studied the distance with narrowed eyes. "Afraid I did, Henry. I just can't stand still for what Ben is up to."

Kleyburg cut the air with an irritated hand. "What is he up to? All Ben wants to do is organize in a common interest. I see it as a good idea. So does Miles Sulivane. So does Jock Dunaway. But you back away from it like it was the devil's own torch. And I can't figure why."

"Because I don't believe any organization necessary," said Howison quietly. "To hear Walrode talk, everybody in the basin is being rustled blind. Well, I'm not. Neither are you. And I don't believe Sulivane or Dunaway are either. Sulivane is such a tight-fisted old blister he'd scream bloody murder at the mere thought of losing a critter. Jock Dunaway is the sort to always string along with the crowd. But me, I want to see some real proof of this rustling, besides just talk."

"Well now," returned Kleyburg with some dry sarcasm. "Seems I heard you admit to a critter of yours being butchered, and then finding the meat in a nester's shed. Isn't that one kind of rustling?"

"Definitely, if true," admitted Howison readily. "Only there are some mighty peculiar angles to that deal."

Kleyburg grunted again. "Only peculiar thing I see is you taking a nester's word against that of three working cowhands. You admit the dead critter and the meat in Tedrow's shed. What more do you want?"

"The real facts, which so far haven't appeared in the open."

"All right," challenged Kleyburg. "If they haven't, and you got some, let's have a look at them. If Tedrow didn't slaughter the critter, who did?"

"Either Jack Labine, Nick Bodie, or Chirk Dennis. Take your choice."

Kleyburg snorted his disbelief. "Next," he said, "you'll be charging that they also planted the meat in Tedrow's shed."

Howison smiled faintly. "Planted is the right word, Henry. Also, yours. Glad to know the possibility had occurred to you."

Kleyburg swung about, his irritation deepening. "Why would they do that?"

"Maybe so Ben could make his rustling claim sound good."

"You even suggest Ben ordered it done?" demanded Kleyburg.

"That's it."

The cattleman shook a forceful head. "I can't swallow that. Ben would never be so dumb."

"Dumb?" murmured Howison. "Seems to have fooled you and Sulivane and Dunaway."

Kleyburg scowled, sucking at his pipe. He found it dead, so searched a pocket for another match.

"Don't make sense," he grumbled finally. "Just plain don't make sense! Either Ben's being rustled, or he ain't. And if he ain't, why would he claim that he is? What would he be trying to prove?"

Howison shrugged. "That's the big answer I'm looking for. I suggest you look for it, too. Before you get roped into this association mess and talked into heading it."

"Told you last night I was capable of thinking for myself," Kleyburg growled. "That's all settled. The four of us — Ben, Sulivane, Dunaway, and me — we took care of that after you and Mallory left."

Howison shook a rueful head. "Sorry to hear Ben's got you where he wants you."

Kleyburg's face darkened under a touch of real anger. "That's got a queer meaning. What are you driving at?"

"Just that he's maneuvered you into the front spot," said Howison simply, "so you'll be the main target of any possible opposition, not him."

Kleyburg's glance searched Howison carefully. "You really believe that, don't you?"

Over at the ranch house a screen door slammed and Sue Kleyburg, dressed for riding, stepped out into the sun. She carried a flat-brimmed Stetson hat and a sack of lunch and had a fleece-lined coat over one arm. She moved across the interval with a free, vigorous stride. Her father watched her approach half-absently, unable to ease his frowning thoughts. Sue, coming up, did not miss her father's mood. She looked at Howison accusingly.

"If you've started a quarrel, maybe we better forget this riding idea."

"No quarrel here," Howison assured her. "And I've already asked your pa about the ride. He said it's all right with him."

"Heck, yes!" rapped Henry Kleyburg

crustily. "Clear out, the pair of you. If you're riding the high country, Dave, better catch up the pinto pony for Sue. It's steadier and more sure-footed than the sorrel filly she sometimes uses."

"Just so," Howison agreed, and proceeded to do it.

The pinto was impatient and eager to run, and as Sue moved off, Howison lingered for a final word with her father.

"I'd sure like to go along with what you want, Henry. But in all good conscience, I can't. Get me right — I'm not being stubborn just for the heck of it."

Kleyburg waved a dismissing hand. "If I wasn't sure of that, you wouldn't be riding with my daughter."

Sue Kleyburg was a full half mile from the ranch house by the time Howison caught up with her. The pinto had made its little run and now was slowed to a jog. When Howison hauled his big buckskin in beside her, Sue eyed him narrowly.

"I've the feeling there's more behind this ride than just the desire for my company. Maybe you better explain."

"All in good time," Howison returned. "Though you may doubt it, your company pleasures me greatly. It always has, even when you get into a fit of sulks, like you've lately been. In short, my good lass, you're the one woman in my life."

His tone was jocular, but his glance wasn't, and under the touch of it, Sue flushed and looked away.

It was, she thought, one of a waning summer's better mornings. The sun was bright, the air was crisp, and all the world was fair. She was glad to be moving through it freely with this lean, brown-faced man riding beside her. Just the same, she decided, it wouldn't do to let him know that. At least, not for a time. So, though it took some effort to maintain it, she kept to her mood of mock severity.

"Call it sulks if you like. Whatever it is, it's your fault. Acting the way you do with Dad — and to Ben Walrode. I just can't understand you."

Howison's grin became a trifle twisted. "Don't always understand myself. But sometimes my hunches pay off. I'm riding one now. So what say we quit scolding and wait for what the day turns up before forming any hard and fast opinions?"

Innately fair-minded, Sue relented. "Sorry," she said. "Sometimes I can be a real stinker. And there's nothing worse than a carping female. A truce?"

Howison's grin widened. "Truce it is."

They held to the town trail for a time, then swung east at a long angle to strike the first lift of the foothills and put the horses to the climb toward the timber country above. These foothills ran away in looping folds, with rounded sweeps of open grassland alternating with narrow gulches and rain-cut gullies that wound down from the heights. On the crest of one rounded lift, Howison pulled up, slacked at ease in his saddle and indicated the cabin that lay below and farther along the basin floor.

"Price Tedrow's layout. Where all the ruckus started. Sometimes I wonder what it is that holds people like Tedrow and his wife to such a place. Just the bare edge past nothing at all to call their own. The world ought to offer something better than that to any man and the woman who shares it with him."

"They are on your land, and you don't mind?" Sue said.

Howison shrugged. "Not hurting me any. And they won't be there forever. They'll stay just until the old, old dream takes hold again. The dream that says over the next ridge, or in the next valley, they'll find what they are searching for. The fabled land of milk and honey. The big rock candy mountain. It won't be there, of course, but the dream says it might be. So they go on looking and hoping. Maybe that's the real reward, the fun of looking and hoping."

"Fun?" murmured Sue. "Or plain brutal hardship?"

"Probably very little of one and a lot of the other," Howison admitted. "Yet they could have what's worth all the hardship. They have each other. Believing in her man, Mrs. Tedrow looked me in the eye and said so. I believed her. She waited for her man to get home from town last night, worried and not too sure he'd make it safely. But when he did and she stood in her doorway and called his name — and the relief that showed in her voice when she knew he was there, safe and sound — well, I felt pretty good about that. Yeah, I felt real good!"

He was smiling again, musing over his rewarding thoughts. Sue threw him a soft, guarded glance.

He sent the buckskin along, facing the lift of the slope fully now, with the pinto scrambling along behind. They reached the first timber and moved into it, where morning's moist, cool breath still hovered. Sue had no idea where they were heading, but Howison did, and presently they reached the spot. Several buzzards, gorged, had roosted overnight in the timber tops above the little meadow. Now they lurched heavily into flight, and a pair of coyotes, late feeding, slipped away into the shadows, fast as furtive ghosts.

The remains of the two year old had been well worked over by both the winged and four-footed scavengers. Howison indicated the shrunken carcass with a lift of his chin.

"Couple of days ago that was one of my best grade beef critters. Now it's just something for the buzzards and coyotes to work on. I expect to collect a fair price for that animal."

"How can you when you don't know who killed it?" Sue asked. "How do you expect to find out for certain?"

"Tracks," Howison told her. "Trail sign. No man can move around in this country without leaving tracks and trail sign. Particularly when he's on a horse. And nobody can leave a spot, any spot, without first coming to that spot. Well, yesterday, when I found this dead critter, I also found and ran down some sign where a rider left the meadow. Now, here, today — you and me — we're going to find where that rider came into this meadow and then we'll backtrack that sign and see where it leads to. Susie, you could be surprised."

She eyed him soberly. "So that's why you wanted me to take this ride with you?"

"Partly," he admitted. "Because, you see, I value your good sense and opinion as well as your company."

She considered this in silence as she twisted in her saddle, looking about the clearing. A buzzard, slower to arouse and leave than its fellows, now lunged from a perch and flapped by close overhead like a somber shroud. It stirred a mustiness in the air, and Sue grimaced in distaste.

"Very well. Let's look for those tracks and see where they lead."

CHAPTER
IV

Tap Geer was a restless soul, full of the spirit that swayed all free and independent men. He liked to go as he pleased and come as he pleased. Time was of little consequence and trails just something to follow, if for no better reason than to find what lay at their far end. Yesterday didn't count because it was already past, and tomorrow hadn't dawned yet. So why worry?

Today was what counted. Yeah — today! This hour, this minute, when morning's sun lay warm across a man's shoulders and his belly was full of venison steak and Barney Tuttle's flapjacks. When the taste of breakfast coffee still lingered rich and savory on a man's tongue and his first Durham cigarette of the day was drawing free and good.

That, mused Tap, as he prowled along the street of Basin City, was how it should be. Yet, this morning he still felt flat and moody and disgruntled.

He climbed the low steps of Luke Casper's Trading Post and settled into one of the half-dozen round-backed chairs scattered along the galleried platform. Luke, short and wide, with a considerable paunch bulging his blue denim, flour-whitened apron, appeared broom in hand and began making leisurely swipes at the platform's dusty length. Coming even with Tap, he paused.

"Kinda unusual, ain't it? You holding down a chair on a fine morning like this? Thought you'd be straddling saddle leather, heading hell-bent for somewhere. What's ailing you?"

Tap scowled grumpily. "Maybe I just want to sit still and mind my own business."

Luke took the hint and moved along, broom swinging more briskly as he made a tart retort.

"Heck with you! Stay there and rot."

Which, brooded Tap darkly, was about all there was left for him to do, seeing what his reputation had become all across Jubilee Basin. All because he had shown the courtesy of the trail to a man who had never done him any wrong, or was likely to. He had treated Jett Chesbro to a drink of coffee and chinned with him for a while about this and that and nothing in particular. But that windy old fool, Buck Pruitt, had to come by with the stage, take a look, and then proceed to spread the word all over. After which Ben Walrode opened his big mouth to make out like Tap Geer had been drinking coffee with the devil himself. And in consequence . . . !

Tap's mournful soliloquy of thought ran out into this vocal expression of growling disgust. Returning along the platform, Luke Casper heard and eyed him closely.

"You sure are full of poison this morning. You hate yourself?"

Tap grinned weakly. Luke was a good guy and a friend.

"Myself — along with some others I could name."

"Like Jack Labine, maybe?" Luke hazarded.

"He's one," Tap nodded. "You heard about it — his deadline talk?"

Luke stepped to the edge of the platform, spat into the street's dust, and turned back.

"I heard. And was I you, I'd kind of take it to heart. About staying this side of Big Stony, I mean. Ain't nothin' south of it for you but trouble."

Luke was right in this, as Tap knew full well, but he was so sore about the whole business, he bristled.

"Maybe you figure I been foolin' around cattle I don't own?"

"Sometimes," returned Luke evenly, "you talk like you didn't have good sense. If I thought that, would you be sittin' here in one of my chairs? You'd be making tracks down that street, and me after you with a pick handle."

"Ben Walrode," declared Tap, "is a liar!"

"That," conceded Luke cautiously, "could be. I ain't sayin' it out loud, understand. But could be. Lots of men are, now and then."

"And should the idea hit real hard, I'll ride south of Big Stony any time I please," Tap vowed.

Luke spat into the street again, then stood for a moment in narrow-eyed thought.

"Me," he propounded slowly, "I'm just a run-of-the-mill, potbellied storekeeper. Still and all, I keep an ear to the ground and sometimes come up with notions that pan out about right. Boy, something is brewing in this basin. I ain't even halfway sure what it is, but it's there just the same. And whatever it is, it'll end up among the big fellers — all too big for you to mix in. So like I tell you, stay this side of Big Stony and don't try and wrastle with somebody you ain't got a chance to handle. That way, you'll live longer."

Having dispensed this bit of wisdom, Luke turned back into his store. Tap set about twisting up another cigarette. The little muslin Durham sack he drew from his shirt pocket was limp and flat, and he had to shake it thoroughly to get enough out of it to make even a half way decent smoke. Gloom settled in again.

Things sure were bad when a man was out of tobacco and didn't have a thin dime in his jeans with which to buy more. He, Tap Geer, needed a riding job, and bad! Where to find one? Dave Howison would probably take him on, just out of friendship, even while not needing another hand. But Tap Geer would never take advantage of that state of affairs, not ever. Not even if he had to go without ever smoking again. Not ever, by jiggers — if he even had to go without eating . . . !

But where else to locate a job? He might have stood a show once with Henry Kleyburg, or Jock Dunaway, or even with that old skinflint, Miles Sulivane, back before Ben Walrode started talking. But now — not a chance with any of them.

From down below town sounded the

clatter of hoofs on the Big Stony bridge and presently a team and spring wagon turned into the street and came along it. Tap's disconsolate glance noted its arrival, but paid little heed until, with the rig drawing closer, he realized who was driving it.

Chirk Dennis!

Tap straightened in his chair, quickening interest and sudden purpose gusting through him. Chirk Dennis, of the Sawbuck outfit! One of Ben Walrode's riders. The ominous gleam in Tap's eyes deepened as the wagon swung in and braked to a halt at the Trading Post hitch rail.

By this time, the morning sun had climbed high enough for the gallery across the store front to throw a band of shadow where Tap's chair stood. Turned lazy in mind and body by the wagon ride in from headquarters, Chirk Dennis was paying little attention to details of the town and was therefore unaware of Tap's presence until, after tying his team, he climbed the steps and found Tap waiting for him at the top of them.

"Mister Dennis, I do declare," greeted Tap, grinning wickedly. "Up and about so early this fine morning. Just where would you be going, Mister Dennis?"

Chirk Dennis was a queer-shaped man. He had narrow shoulders that sloped down into an equally narrow torso that widened into heavy hips and legs. He was habitually surly, dull of wit, and inclined to a casual brutality. Now, though startled, he held his ground and returned stare for stare.

"What's it to you?" he demanded thickly.

"Plenty!" Tap returned crisply. "Last night I was told Big Stony Creek was a deadline for me. I wasn't to get south of it because that was all Sawbuck country. Well, me — I figure there's two sides to any deadline and right now you're on the wrong side. So climb into your little old wagon and head right back across Big Stony to Sawbuck country where you belong."

Chirk Dennis blinked and stared a little harder.

"You crazy, Geer? Boss sent me to town for a load of grub and stuff. Get out of my way!"

"Unh-uh!" differed Tap. "You're over the deadline, Dennis. Hightail back across it while you're able to."

Again Chirk Dennis blinked, slowly assimilating the weight of Tap's ultimatum. When it finally registered fully, he mumbled angrily and swung an arm against Tap's chest to brush him aside.

Tap didn't brush. Anticipating some such reaction, he was braced for it. He threw a shoulder into Dennis and drove him stumbling down the steps. Aware that he was now fully committed, and wanting it so, Tap followed, charging joyously to battle.

"Git along little dogey!" he whooped.

Because of his ungainly build, Chirk Dennis looked clumsy, but was not entirely so. Regaining his balance, he sidestepped Tap's rush and landed a wallop under the ear that made Tap see skyrockets and sent him rolling in the street's dust.

More surprised than hurt, Tap was swiftly up again and whirling back to the fray, though not quite as headlong as before. So it was that when Dennis launched another roundhouse swing, Tap was able to duck under it and sink a driving fist into the Sawbuck rider's midriff.

It was a good punch, which wrung a grunt from Dennis and bent him over. Tap made the most of this opportunity by digging a set of hard, chopping knuckles to his man's nose, which brought forth both a gush of crimson and a bawl of torrid profanity. It also brought Dennis lunging in.

Tap tried to stand him off with another

smash to the face, but the punch landed high, skidding off the top of Dennis's bullet head. Before Tap could recover, Dennis had hold of him and Tap found himself in definite trouble.

Hooked to those narrow shoulders, Chirk Dennis's arms were long and sinewy and snaky strong when they wound about a man. And those spread and heavy legs made for a foundation of power Tap couldn't hope to match in this chest-to-chest business. Dennis lifted him clear off his feet and threw him against the hitch rail with a force that jackknifed him over it. So again Tap found himself rolling in the dust, almost under the hoofs of the startled Sawbuck team.

He scrambled clear and made it to his feet, the hitch rail between him and Dennis. Now he was quite sure he had bit himself off a considerable mouthful. He also knew he had started something he must now see to a finish, regardless. If he didn't, then he would have to sneak out of Jubilee Basin like a whipped coyote. Deep down beneath the carefree exterior he showed the world, there was a considerable streak of tough metal in Tap Geer. Also, when he got mad — and he was that now — he got smart.

He circled the Sawbuck rig and came at Chirk Dennis once more, but with the full width of the street to maneuver in. One thing was very definite: it wouldn't do to let Dennis get hold of him, or try to match brute strength with brute strength. This, he knew, was exactly what Dennis would try to bring about. He read the thought and purpose in Dennis's mean and glowering eyes, saw also the confidence the man felt. The next time they came close, Tap decided, Dennis would be grabbing for him, rather than throwing a punch. So he set out to profit accordingly.

Back in the Trading Post, Luke Casper had heard the Sawbuck wagon haul up out front, but not until the burst of cursing erupted from Chirk Dennis did he know any concern. Now he moved to see what was going on. At the same time, Milt Shannon hove into sight in front of the courthouse with nothing in particular on his mind beyond a look at another fine, late-summer morning. However, when his casual, swinging glance picked up the disturbance up the street, he hurried along that way.

Neither Tap Geer nor Chirk Dennis noted the sheriff's approach, but Luke Casper did and cautioned him with a lifted hand. Shannon scrambled up over the end of the platform, mumbling.

"What the devil's it all about, Luke?"

"Little argument over a deadline, I think," Luke murmured. "I'd guess Tap Geer is out to set somebody right on that particular point. Also, I suggest you stay out of it, Milt, unless it turns into something more serious than fists."

"You're probably right," agreed Shannon.

Tap Geer had eyes and ears for nothing or no one except the man in front of him. He moved in on Dennis, weaving a little, circling a little, first this way, then back again, always edging closer. He slid his feet through the dust, keeping them well under him and set for the big effort when opportunity offered.

Chirk Dennis was equally absorbed. He watched unwinking, measuring the shortening distance, set and eager to get his hands on Tap again, vowing darkly that when he did he would do more than just throw him over the hitch rail. He would break his back!

There was a pressure in this maneuvering, a pressure that built up in both men. To Tap it was a power couched and coiled in his right shoulder, ready to explode. In Chirk Dennis it was that almost atavistic hunger to rip and tear, to break and stomp down. And it grew so strong in Dennis it betrayed him. For as Tap made another feinting shuffle, Dennis lunged for him, arms spread and reaching, fingers hooked.

This was the move Tap had waited for. He stepped between those reaching arms, feet solidly under him and knees slightly sprung to get full, lifting leverage behind the savage smash he aimed at Chirk Dennis's body. It was a wicked blow, wickedly planned, wickedly landed, and it carried every ounce of weight and power Tap could put into it. It caught Chirk Dennis coming in, caught him squarely under the heart, and for a moment virtually destroyed him.

His jaw wobbled and dropped, a gasping groan bursting from him. His arms fell loose and useless at his sides. He rocked back and forth like a tree about to fall under a woodman's ax.

Tap stayed with his man, picked another target and hit it — Dennis's open, sagging jaw. Dennis spun half around in a loose, knee-crumpling turn and went down full length in the dust. Carried away by the fever of combat, Tap stood over him for a long moment, waiting for him to get up. But he realized presently that Dennis wasn't going to get up, at least not right away. Then the reaction set in.

It had not been a thing of any great duration, but there had been a couple of explosive moments that burned up plenty of energy. Tap's knees wobbled a little, so he backed up to lean against the hitch rail, gulping hungrily for air. Sweat broke and trickled down his face.

It was some little time before Chirk Dennis began to stir and thrash around, began to mumble and curse. He lifted finally to one elbow, then to a knee, but here he wavered and fell over on his face again. He cursed some more, spat out a blob of dust and curdled blood, then made another try at getting up. He did better this time, achieving a sitting position, which he held while staring around with blurred and stupid gaze.

He had no gun on him, nor did Tap. But slung in its leather boot behind the seat of the spring wagon was a .44 Winchester. Across this basin range it was a general thing to carry a rifle in such fashion in a wagon or buckboard on the chance of knocking off a marauding coyote or even a lobo wolf, foraging down from some covert high in the Sentinels. Or perhaps a sick or accident-crippled beef animal, or a horse, needed to be put out of its misery. So no one present gave the weapon a second thought. No one except Chirk Dennis. But within him, as full realization of what had happened seeped through his dazed, stumbling mind, a feral cunning began to grow.

He played it cagey, even after his scrambled wits began to work and he had much of his breath back from that savage belt in the midriff. He scrubbed some of the blood from his face and sat with hanging head, apparently too used up to make a further move. But all the time he was calculating how far Tap Geer was from him and how close he was to the wagon — and that rifle. It figured, he decided viciously, as a pretty good gamble.

Again he scrubbed a hand across his face and shook his head as though fighting his way through a cloud of cobwebs. He lurched to his feet, caught at the wagon wheel to steady himself, leaned hard against it as though in need of support. Then he made his grab.

He had the rifle clear of the boot before Tap Geer was fully aware of the move and the intent. Luke Casper and Milt Shannon were equally off guard, and Luke's yell of warning was just forming in his throat when Tap understood and threw himself at

Dennis, coldly desperate. Dennis brought the rifle up, hip high and level, at the same time swinging the lever to jack a cartridge from magazine to chamber.

The instant that lever fully closed, Tap knew Chirk Dennis held crashing death in his hands. And how far the distance he must cover to head it off . . . Three yards, four yards . . . ? He saw the muzzle of the gun coming into line, and he struck at it, reaching out to his utmost. His hand met the hard steel of the rifle barrel, deflected it slightly, barely ahead of the hard, flat report. He felt the hot breath of the weapon, but not the strike of lead tearing at his vitals. God's luck — not that . . . !

Then he had full grip on the gun, fighting Chirk Dennis for possession of it.

Earlier, he had known anger. But it was nothing beside the wild, destroying fury that gripped him now, giving him strength to jam Dennis against the wagon, which now jerked back and forth as the team, spooked by the smash of gun report so close, was trampling and swinging, near to pulling loose from their halter tie.

Tap got the rifle twisted crossways against Chirk Dennis's chest, bent his man backwards, then twice drove a knee into him, weakening him. Dennis lost his grip on the gun, and Tap threw it clear, after which he set out to beat Dennis's head off with a pair of vengeful, hammering fists. He was still working at this, clubbing his man without letup, not knowing that only the support of the wagon was keeping Dennis erect, when Milt Shannon got hold of him and pulled him away. Whereupon Dennis slid down into the dust, battered senseless.

"That ought to be enough, Tap," said Shannon. "You could hit him with a pick handle now and he wouldn't feel it. Yeah, you've curried him enough."

"Never enough!" fumed Tap wildly. "He tried to gun me — kill me!"

"Darn near did, too," Shannon agreed laconically. "Better put out that hole in your shirt before it burns you up."

Tap became aware of the acrid smell of scorched and charring cloth. He looked down. A hole in a loose fold of his shirt just above his hip was sending forth a wispy curl of smoke, while the smoldering edges of the hole were widening steadily. He beat out this spreading char, gulping at the realization of how close a thing it had been. That close . . . ! Close enough for the flame of a gun to set his shirt afire.

Tap looked down at his prone adversary

with a renewed surge of anger.

"I oughta stomp him! Dirty sneak — I oughta stomp him!"

"Maybe," said Milt Shannon meagerly. "Only you're not about to. Go somewhere and cool off. I'll take care of him."

"No!" argued Tap vehemently, "I will. That Sawbuck outfit started this thing, and I'll finish it. They threw a deadline at me, so they get it right back in their faces. Soon as this jigger is able to see straight, he goes right back like he came — with an empty wagon. That's it!"

"All right — all right, if you want it so," conceded Shannon with some impatience. "But right now you go some place. Clear out!"

About now this seemed to make sense, Tap decided, for his knees were turning rubbery again. He shuffled over to the platform and sat on the edge of it, taking stock. Again he looked at the hole in his shirt and probed at it with a finger. Maybe, he thought, with sudden worry, that slug did take a chunk of hide off him and he hadn't got around to feeling it yet. The hole, however, was no deeper than his shirt. But, son-of-a-gun — it sure had been a close one!

A hand fell on his shoulder, and he

looked up to see Luke Casper offering a bottle.

"Take a drag," ordered Luke gruffly. "Take a good one. Bumptious young bucko! Figure yourself a regular wildcat now, I suppose. Well, you near got yourself killed. Go ahead — take a drag."

Tap did so. The liquor hit bottom and burned away most of the flutterbugs chasing around in his stomach. He sighed and took a second drag before surrendering the bottle. Then he spoke up grimly.

"Dennis came to town for grub and stuff, so he said. But he goes home without any. I hate to do you out of the business, Luke, but today he takes home an empty wagon."

Luke shrugged. "All right with me. I'll still live. But you can't keep this thing up forever, you know."

"Not forever," Tap admitted. "But for today, I do. This is my day to howl, and I'm making it loud enough for Ben Walrode and his whole outfit to hear me. I can't explain it good, Luke, but it means an awful lot to me. I just got to make it stick — today."

"Sure," soothed Luke. "I know. But I still say — don't try and play it too big, kid. You just don't pack enough weight."

Milt Shannon had Chirk Dennis back on his feet again, but in very shaky condition. The sheriff called to Luke Casper.

"A little of that stuff in the bottle would do some good here, too. That is, if you figure it worth it."

"Anything to clear the air," answered Luke. "Come and get it."

"Honest whiskey's too good for that hombre," grumbled Tap malevolently. "Rat poison would be more like it."

Chirk Dennis sucked greedily at the bottle, but put out with no argument at all when Shannon told him to get in the wagon and head out. Dennis was a thoroughly beaten and used up individual, and for this day at least, wanted no more of the thunder and lightning he had run into. Milt Shannon untied the team for him and watched the wagon roll out of town. As he brought the bottle back to Luke Casper, the sheriff shook his head and complained plaintively.

"What's happened to this range, anyhow? Why can't people get along peaceable? Everything was moving nice and quiet. Now, the way things are going, I dunno!" He shook his head again.

Luke Casper stared off into the distance for a little time before giving slow answer.

"Quit bellyachin', Milt. Because you won't find no sympathy around me. Any man who keeps straddlin' the fence the way you've been doing is bound to come up with a sore crotch. And it's all your own fault. You can't be half this and half that. At your job, no man can. To get results you got to be one thing or the other so people can put their finger on you. If you want to see this basin peaceful, then you got to quit playin' politics and make it so."

Luke Casper went inside. Milt Shannon returned slowly to his office, shoulders hunched, head bent in uncomfortable thought.

Tap Geer remained sitting in the sun, counting his sore spots and reliving the moments of the fight. He knew the lid was completely off now, but he didn't care. For this moment at least, he owned the street and he was relaxed and content. For that matter, he felt downright happy . . . !

CHAPTER

V

The headquarters of Ben Walrode's Sawbuck outfit stood on a low benchland south of Chancellor Peak, overlooking a sweep of land that stretched away to where the southern tip of the Cold River Rim and the misty blue bulk of the Sentinels met and blended in a wild, broken spread of lava pothole country. The northern border of Sawbuck range was Big Stony Creek and on the west it was the stage road from the Big Stony crossing to where the road dipped into Horsehead Canyon. South lay a far run of government grass that Walrode used and made a show of claiming.

On a rocky shoulder of Chancellor Peak, about a half mile above Sawbuck headquarters, Dave Howison and Sue Kleyburg sat their saddles, studying the layout below. Easily traceable in its winding, yet certain way, through scrub brush and patches of thinning timber, ran a down-sloping trail, lately used.

Giving his companion time to get the picture and draw conclusions of her own, Howison turned to her.

"Well, Susie, there it is. What do you think?"

"I certainly can't argue the evidence of my own eyes," admitted Sue soberly. "If only," she added, "the why of it made sense."

"Just give Ben a little more time," Howison said. "The Tedrow affair could be merely an early move in some bigger scheme."

"If," went on Sue slowly, "it is as it seems, it certainly is brazen. Because whoever is responsible must certainly realize what the hoof sign along this trail suggests. It's hard to see them being that careless."

"Yes — and no," Howison said. "There's this to remember. Price Tedrow is a lone nester in a land of cattlemen, who at best never see anything good about one of his kind. To them he is a shiftless mendicant, a range spoiler, a natural born thief, and a liar by choice. Last night at the meeting Miles Sulivane proclaimed that he'd never seen a nester who wasn't a liar and a thief, any time opportunity offered. Ben could have figured things that way, with no one taking Tedrow's word against that of three well-known Sawbuck hands. My seeing it differently is the only reason any argument at all showed up. No, it was a good gamble, and Ben took it."

"Hoping to gain what?"

Howison shrugged. "Too early to tell. But he's up to something."

He marked the increasing tilt of the afternoon sun. As he had promised when asking Sue along, they had made a day of it, carefully working out and backtracking a trail from the site of the slow-elking, a trail that had led them to this spot, and would have, had they continued to follow, taken them to that headquarters below.

Along the way they had stopped at midday at a spring-fed glade in the timber. After loosening cinches and letting the mounts graze, Howison put together a small fire and cooked coffee, while Sue laid out the lunch she had brought. It was a pleasant spot to spend a lazy hour, with all the fine, free flavor of this high timber country around them, and for this little time Sue pushed aside the shadow of troubled thought and let her usual brightness of spirit take over. Now, however, with the full significance of the trail they had followed lying too plain to be ignored, her mood was once more sober and subdued.

At the distant mouth of Horsehead Canyon, a thin haze of dust lifted and moved north along the road toward town. Under the dust and made toylike by distance, Buck Pruitt's stage and team of six were headed for Basin City. And down below, pulling away from Sawbuck headquarters, a spring wagon angled out across the basin toward that same road.

Sue stirred, restless in her saddle.

"What now, David?"

"Home," said Howison. "By way of town. The stage could be carrying some mail."

They cut back around the flank of the peak, crossing the headwaters of Big Stony and dropping steadily downgrade along the roll of the foothills to the level country beyond. It was close to sundown when they reached town and hauled up at the Trading Post. Going in, they caught Luke Casper in the act of sorting out the contents of the thin mail pouch Buck Pruitt had left with him.

"Evening, folks," he greeted. "Here's a little bit of something, but not much of anything. Your dad's Stockman's Journal and a dress catalog for you and your mother, Sue. Dave, you draw a blank."

Howison tipped a shoulder. "About as

usual. What's new around town, if anything?"

"Mite of excitement this morning," Luke said. "Tap Geer kinda raised a little breeze."

"So-o!" Howison showed a quick interest. "What did Tap do?"

"Well for one thing," related Luke, obviously relishing the opportunity of going over it again, "he larruped the everlasting daylights out of Chirk Dennis. Yes, sir. For a wild-eyed minute or two he sure kept the flies off Chirk. Can't ever remember seeing friend Tap so wound up. Most generally he's happy-go-lucky and almost too easygoing for his own good."

"What set him off?"

"That deadline business Sawbuck laid out against him. Chirk Dennis showed up in a spring wagon after a load of grub and such. Tap braced him right out there on my steps and wouldn't let him pass, tellin' him there were two sides to any deadline and that any Sawbuck hand showing up in town was on the wrong side of it. So he suggested Chirk get back on his own side, muy pronto! Chirk, he set out to argue the point, and the fireworks started. It was quite a go while it lasted, but it ended with Tap convincing Dennis — the hard way. So Chirk went home with an empty wagon."

Howison chuckled. "Good for Tap!"

Sue Kleyburg's reaction was otherwise. "I think it was ridiculous," she exclaimed. "Didn't anyone try to stop them? What about Sheriff Shannon?"

"Milt, he came along and watched," said Luke. "He didn't mess in until Tap was really curryin' Dennis after Dennis tried to use a gun on him."

"Gun?" Howison sobered.

Luke explained that part of the affair. "It was close. Shot a hole in Tap's shirt."

"You see!" flared Sue at Howison. "Tap might have been killed. You men! Worse than children. Forever starting a fight over the silliest things. Just what, I'd like to know, did Tap Geer prove by acting so?"

"To himself, probably a lot," Howison defended. "A man was made to stand on his own two feet, not crawl to anybody. Least of all to Ben Walrode and company. Tap was just proving to the whole wide world that he was a man. Where is he now, Luke?"

"Wouldn't know. Off chasing his shadow somewhere, I expect. He's a restless rascal. Rode out of town about noon."

"Put you out of some business, didn't he, handling Dennis the way he did?"

Luke shrugged a meaty shoulder.

"I can stand it. Tap worried some about that, after he'd cooled off. I told him to forget it, as I don't go for any of this dead-line business myself. They threw it at Tap. He's got the right to throw it back."

From the street came the soft, dust-muffled mutter of arriving hoofs, the jingle of harness, and the dry squeal of a hickory brake-block tightening against an iron shod wheel. Also sounded the growl of a gravelly voice and the thump of bootheels crossing the platform outside. Then it was the high shape of Jack Labine filling the doorway, with Nick Bodie at his heels. Labine's gravelly, irritating voice hit through the warm gloom of the room.

"Casper, when the hell did you figure you didn't need any more business from Sawbuck?"

Luke Casper bristled. "That time could be right now, Labine, unless you watch your tongue. There's a lady present."

Coming from the street's sundown light into ever-deepening shadow, in addition to being somewhat blinded by his own dark anger, Labine had not immediately noticed the presence of Dave Howison and Sue Kleyburg. Now that he did, he tempered his words somewhat.

"Sorry. Didn't notice at first. Kind of

dark in here." But the combative rasp returned as he faced Casper again. "I sent a man in this morning after a load of supplies. He came back with an empty wagon. Something wrong with Sawbuck credit?"

"No. But something wrong if Chirk Dennis says I'm in any way responsible," retorted Luke. "He never ordered anything from me. Fact is, he never came inside that door or spoke a word to me. So, what's your gripe? I didn't run him out of town."

"But you must have known what he was after."

"Not me," differed Luke curtly. "I'm no mind reader. Neither am I out to fight any battles for Sawbuck. I understand you set up a deadline. Well, that knife can cut both ways, and it's your own fault if you run up against the sharp edge of it. Now, if you've come after what Chirk Dennis didn't get, name it and we'll do business."

Dave Howison had Sue Kleyburg by the elbow, steering her toward the door. He thought Labine meant to ignore him. But the spleen in the Sawbuck foreman was rampant and now he swung a hot-eyed glance.

"If you rate that fellow Geer a friend of yours, Howison, you better cool him off. Else Sawbuck will. He's gettin' a little outsized for his own good."

"Tap's my friend, all right," returned Howison bluntly. "Told you that before. Who hits him, hits me. Best remember it, Labine. And something else for you to do. Tell Ben Walrode he owes me a prime two-year-old beef steer, which I'll be around to collect for. He'll know what I mean, just like you do!"

Sue Kleyburg said nothing until they were outside and in their saddles again. Then she spoke with plenty of force. "Do you like trouble? Must you always invite it?"

Howison grinned faintly and shook his head. "Susie, girl — I never hunt trouble. But sometimes it's pushed at me. Also, it ruffles my roach just to look at some people. Jack Labine happens to be one of such."

"Why not put the blame where it belongs?" insisted Sue. "From what I've heard so far, Tap Geer is the one at fault. He started things. Do you always have to take his part?"

"I do when such as Labine starts making bully-puss talk. And Tap's my good friend. I believe in sticking by my friends."

"Even when they are in the wrong?"

Howison considered this for a time in

silence as they rode past Jim Treft's livery stable at the edge of town. From the dark mouth of the stable runway Treft's white-eyed shepherd dog barked fitfully. Howison's buckskin swung a little wide, and the move stirred its rider to speech.

"Tap wasn't in the wrong. He has just as much right to lay out a deadline as Ben Walrode has. And that is what caused today's ruckus, the deadline business that Walrode started. You heard Luke Casper say so."

"Suppose I did," persisted Sue spiritedly. "But it is one thing to deny entry to land that you own, and something else to try and deny another person the right to enter town. No one can do that."

"Not unless you can make it stick," chuckled Howison. "Which Tap did. And besides, remember the deadline Sawbuck threw at Tap called for everything south of Big Stony. There's a lot of free land down there that Ben Walrode has no more right to than I have. Yet he'd try and keep Tap off it. So — what's your answer?"

"Simply that you're stubborn enough to stick up for Tap Geer, right or wrong, I suppose."

Howison's musing smile became a nod. "That's about it. I might give Tap a little hell, a talking to now and then. But any place out in public, I'm for the boy all the way."

"So what it really amounts to," charged Sue tartly, "is that you're for anyone who is against Ben Walrode."

"That's coming close," Howison admitted.

They rode in lengthening silence, their horses breasting an ever-deepening tide of twilight shadow that filled all of the basin's far reaches. Against the rioting crimson of a sunset sky the Cold River Rim was a purple-black barrier. East, the Sentinels were turning a smoky blue, and high up on old Chancellor, touched by a final flare of sunlight, an aspen thicket burned purest gold.

A little breeze stole along the darkening earth, and Sue's glance swung to mark all of this old and well-remembered scene.

"I love it!" she burst out abruptly. "It's my world. I was born here, and I never want to leave it. And I've no patience with those who would spoil it with silly arguments and enmities. You hear me, David Howison?"

"I hear," Howison answered. "But remember it's my world, too — and I'm not out to spoil it. Neither am I going to sit still while somebody else does. You can tell that to Ben Walrode, the next time you see him."

It was well past full dark by the time they rode in at Kleyburg headquarters. Lamplight shone in ranch house and bunkhouse windows. Carrying a shade of jocular relief, Henry Kleyburg's deep growl came out of the shadow by the corrals.

"You two sure did make a day of it. I was beginning to wonder if you hadn't decided to run off for good."

Sue flared instantly. "Dad, don't you be an idiot, too!"

Howison's drawl was touched with slow amusement. "I think our young lady is out of patience with all male critters, Henry. She'll probably tell you why. And thanks, Susie, for going along."

"Light down and eat, Dave," Kleyburg invited.

"Some other time." Howison was already swinging the buckskin away. "Woody Biggs will be fretting if I don't show."

While her father cared for her pony, Sue Kleyburg crossed the dark interval to the ranch house, her step a trifle weary — not from the hours she had spent in the saddle, as she was a vigorous girl full of boundless health and well used to long saddle travel. But for some reason the day had drained her emotionally.

In the warm, food-fragrant kitchen, her

mother eyed her shrewdly. "Child, you've a lot on your mind. But I'll wait until you've had supper to hear about it. Glad you went with David?"

Sue answered slowly. "Yes — and no. Oh, Mother — why can't men grow up, instead of acting like quarrelsome small boys?"

Mrs. Kleyburg smiled wisely. "Because, my dear, in some ways they never entirely outlive that age. Which is something we women must recognize and learn to accept. Perhaps it is one of the reasons we come to cherish them so."

"Not me!" declared Sue fiercely. "There's times when I could wring their wretched necks!"

She felt better after she had washed up and had supper. Her father came in and sat quietly with his pipe while she ate, but she could see he was impatient to hear about her day. He finally could hold in no longer.

"Sue, it's been my feeling Dave Howison had two reasons for taking you on that ride. First, because you're a pretty girl he's fond of. The other was to show you something. Right?"

Sue nodded. "I wouldn't know about the first, but you're right about the second."

Then she told of the trail that had been so carefully backtracked and where it led. Her mother nodded triumphantly.

"There it is, Henry. Proving what David and I have argued right along. Ben Walrode is up to something, and you shouldn't let him lead you into his scheme, whatever it is."

Kleyburg grunted. "He's not leading me any place I don't want to go. Far as that trail is concerned, I can't see where it proves anything in particular. What's wrong with a man taking a ride through the Sentinels? Suppose we agree that somebody from Sawbuck did ride through that way and stumbled on to a Bar 88 steer that had been slow-elked. So they set out to run down where the meat had gone to and found it hanging in a nester's shed. What," he ended, "could be simpler than that?"

"It's just a little too simple," countered his wife stoutly. "And comes up against the fact that Price Tedrow had nothing at all to do with it."

"You'd take the word of a shirt-tail nester against that of three regular cow-hands?"

"Against that of certain cowhands, yes, I would. In particular I'd believe Mrs.

Tedrow. I met her in town one day. Nester's wife or not, she showed me a dignity that could not be mistaken. Henry, there's pride and honesty in that woman. She's no thief, and she wouldn't remain in the same house with any man who was."

Henry Kleyburg got to his feet and took a restless, grumbling turn up and down the room.

"How can you be sure what she thinks, or claims? You haven't seen her since this thing happened."

"That's true. But I know what she told David Howison. He believes her, so I do, too."

"Which puts Dave Howison and Ben Walrode on opposite sides of the fence," Kleyburg growled. "Thinking about it, I guess they always have been. Maybe because of that, Howison is believing only what he wants to believe."

"That's unfair, Henry," differed Mrs. Kleyburg sharply. "You're the one set to see only one side."

The cattleman paced the room, scrubbing an irritated hand across his face. He looked at Sue.

"You know them both, Howison and Ben. You've ridden with each of them, and you've sat on the porch with each of them and watched the moon come up. What do you think?"

"At the moment, that they're both stubborn as mules," Sue declared with some vigor. "And if some sense isn't knocked into the pair of them, worse things than a slow-elking will take place in Jubilee Basin."

Her father's glance sharpened. "Maybe something besides running down a trail happened today?"

Sue nodded. "In town." She told what took place in the Trading Post, what Luke Casper said about Tap Geer's ruckus with Chirk Dennis, and what Jack Labine had to say when he and Nick Bodie showed up. "All of which was bad enough," Sue added. "But then Dave said flatly that Tap Geer was a friend of his and that he stood behind Tap, no matter what. It was actually a threat, the way Dave spoke to that Jack Labine. I declare, I don't know what's come over him; he never used to be so ready to fight. Later, when I said I thought Tap Geer was in the wrong, running Chirk Dennis out of town, he just shrugged and insisted it still didn't matter. Tap Geer was his friend and, right or wrong, he'd stand by him."

"That, too, I admire in David Howison,"

defended Mrs. Kleyburg. "He's a steadfast man. Instead of trying to change him, Henry, why not make Ben Walrode do the changing? And discourage his idea of organizing to harass people and mind everybody's business instead of his own?"

"Too late," rumbled Kleyburg. "That's already decided and settled on. I wouldn't want to discourage it, as there's nothing about it to harm any honest person."

"If it sets off trouble, as it seems likely to, it could hurt a lot of people," said Mrs. Kleyburg, sober worry in her eyes. "I remember so well our early years together, Henry. Some of them were tragic ones, as you recall, when men died violently because certain other men were out to run things to suit their own ends. I'd hoped we'd outlived such times, and I never want to see them return. But they could if Ben Walrode is allowed to set up deadlines and send his men out to plant false evidence and bully lone, defenseless, harmless nester folk. Yes, they could come again, and, Henry, I don't want you mixed up in — in them." Her voice broke slightly as she finished.

Kleyburg stopped his prowling and stood beside her, dropping a gentle, reassuring hand on her shoulder.

"I'll take care of that, Mother," he promised gruffly. "I'll hold Ben down. Don't you worry."

He turned to his daughter again. "Sue, I haven't had your flat-out opinion yet. And I want it. Don't sidestep this time. Who is it? Dave Howison or Ben Walrode? You got to face up to the word of one or the other of those two men. Who do you believe?"

It was something Sue had been debating with herself all day. And right from the first she knew the answer. Perversely enough, however, she didn't want to admit it flat out, even to herself. For no good reason other than a vast impatience with both men whose enmity and differences threatened to upset her steady, pleasant world. There were deeper reasons, too — worry over the ominous shadows beginning to shroud the outcome, and a fear that nagged her.

The impact of her father's glance held her, and the demand in it was not to be denied.

"All right, Dad," she sighed. "If you must know the man — I rode with him today."

CHAPTER

VI

It was a morning on which three separate men rose earlier than usual, made restless by thoughts of problems to be faced. At Bar 88, Dave Howison had a fire going and coffee on when Woody Biggs came shuffling into the kitchen, grumpy and scolding in the yellow lamplight.

"Get away from that stove. Handlin' a skillet is my chore around this layout. What's the idea hurryin' the day this way? What's so all-fired important?"

Howison grinned. "Too many questions to answer so early in the morning. Go wash your face and you'll feel better."

Woody snorted, crossed to the bench by the door, poured water and dipped in, sputtering and blowing. After which, over a busy towel, he eyed Howison accusingly.

"You're up to something. What?"

"Got to locate a friend and have a talk."

Woody grunted and hung up the towel.

"Sounds phony. What friend?"

"Tap Geer."

"What you want to see him about?"

Howison told of affairs as he had heard them last evening from Luke Casper. A thin chuckle seeped from Woody.

"So Tap run Chirk Dennis out of town, did he? Good for Tap! Next time he comes by I stake him to a free meal. What you aimin' to do with him?"

"Warn him not to stick his neck out too far. He might be able to handle Chirk Dennis, but he'd be way overmatched should he tangle with Jack Labine or Nick Bodie."

Woody considered this for a moment, then nodded. "A mean pair. See you don't get into trouble with them yourself."

Howison gave no answer to that, heading out under the chill morning stars to grain the buckskin while Woody put breakfast together.

In another ranch kitchen, Henry Kleyburg also ate early breakfast, then hitched a team to a buckboard and headed for town. And in town it was Sheriff Milt Shannon who came down from his room to prowl the street while waiting for the hotel breakfast gong to sound and to watch the dawn fire stream in past Chancellor Peak.

Never a cheerful, out-giving man, Milt Shannon was even more morose than usual, finding himself soundly caught on the well-known horns of a dilemma. He was recalling a line of reading he had once run across. "To be or not to be?" Apparently someone else had once faced such a problem. Now, he mused sourly, it was his own.

Either to be complete master of the office he held, or to surrender much of its authority to this association thing Ben Walrode was cooking up, that was the all of it. One thing or the other. Sheriff in fact or in name only.

Long committed to, and dominated by, the use of practical politics, he now knew a nagging awareness of the true import of the oath of office as he had taken it, and a furtive shame stirred as he considered how far he had strayed from its plainly stated tenets. Stirring also was a small voice of pride, once reasonably full and commanding, but which, down across years of official indolence and softened purpose, had become somewhat atrophied.

It was, he brooded darkly, all very well for Ben Walrode to glibly state what he and others intended to do in helping him fulfill the duties of his office. Yeah, that was easy talk to make and smooth to listen to. Henry Kleyburg had said approximately the same thing, and, being a sincere man, no doubt meant it rightly. Ben Walrode, however, was a different basket of snakes. You never knew for sure what Ben was really up to until it was too late to do anything about it in case you didn't approve.

The easiest way out was, of course, dodging and ducking, riding the fence, playing politics up to the hilt, deciding where the political weight lay, then bowing to it, even though the true obligations of his office suffered. That was how it had been. But now . . . !

The breakfast gong beat out its mellow summons, and Shannon went in and ate, though not with his usual relish. When he returned to the street and moved slowly along, it was to find Henry Kleyburg pulled up in front of his office in a buckboard, basking in the first full flare of morning's sun. Kleyburg indicated the seat beside him.

"Come get some of this sunshine, Milt. Before too long we'll be missing it, as there's the feel of the rougher seasons in the wind. Yeah, climb in while we air our minds a little."

With no legitimate excuse for declining, Shannon took the proffered seat, covering a vague stir of uneasiness by selecting a cigar, carefully paring the tip of it and with equal care getting it alight and drawing fully. Henry Kleyburg had a pipe between his teeth. Now he removed it and spoke slowly.

"Been wondering if we weren't a mite hasty the other night, Milt."

"How do you mean?" Shannon asked. "Hasty about what?"

"Being so certain Tedrow did that slow-elking, and letting it muddy up our thinking, maybe."

"You mean you figure he didn't do it, after all?"

Kleyburg nodded. "Something along that line," he admitted gruffly. "Let's say I'm not as sure about it as I was."

"Well then," Shannon said, "if he didn't do it, who did, and why?"

"That," said Kleyburg, "is what I want to find out. Somebody is lying. I think we should drive out to Sawbuck and have another talk with Ben Walrode."

"Why with Ben?" Shannon was still wary. "What good will that do?"

"Maybe none at all, maybe a lot," Kleyburg growled. "Anyway, I'm on my way there now, and you'd better come along." He turned his head, and his glance was stern. "I hate being played for a sucker, Milt. And if that's how it's been, somebody is due to hear about it. You with me?"

Shannon shrugged. There was no way out.

"All right."

Kleyburg kicked off the brake, stirred his team to motion.

When Dave Howison told Woody Biggs of his intention to hunt up Tap Geer, he spoke the truth. It was, however, only part of his plans for the day — a lesser part. Right now, as he sent the buckskin quick-footing south along the base of the foothills, his immediate destination was Sawbuck headquarters.

Town lay well to his right, and by the time he drew even with it, the sun's first rays were striking up glints from its windows. But here, where he rode, close beneath the lift of the hills, moist, chill shadow still held, and the buckskin moved through this with a willing vigor.

When he crossed Big Stony Creek half a mile below its emergence from its canyon's mouth, he startled some white faces from a little willow swamp. All of these cattle carried Ben Walrode's Sawbuck iron, and all were in good shape. Howison looked them over, then nodded to himself.

"Any one of them will do, Ben," he murmured. "One of them for that two year old of mine. That will be the deal, like it or not!"

He came in on Sawbuck headquarters from the lower basin side and was unnoticed until he sent the buckskin past the corner of the ranch house and over to the corrals, where a stir of activity was taking place.

In a corral, Jack Labine was up on a big, hammer-headed chestnut gelding, working the kinks out of it. The horse was fighting back with twisting, grunting lunges, but Labine, a top hand in a rough saddle, was making the ride without too much concern.

An interested spectator, Ben Walrode was perched on the fence, and Nick Bodie, afoot in the corral at its far side, watched from there. Walrode had his back to Howison and Labine was intent on the chore at hand, so it was Nick Bodie who noted Howison's approach and called a guttural warning.

Ben Walrode turned, stared, then dropped to the ground. Sounding another warning to Labine, Bodie crossed the corral quickly, cleared the fence, and stood beside his boss. Finally alert, Labine shucked out of the saddle and came to join the others. In the way these three now lined up to face him, shoulder to shoulder, lay a suspicion, a challenge, and an uneasy hostility that moved Howison to sarcastic comment.

"What is it, Ben? You expecting an Indian uprising?"

Walrode tried to pass it off with a shrug. "That wouldn't surprise me any more than seeing you here." The retort was heavy. "Maybe you got something on your mind?"

Howison thrust his chin at Labine. "Didn't he give you the word? I told him to."

"What word?"

"That I'd be around to collect for the beef critter you owe me."

Walrode's eyes narrowed. "I don't know what you're driving at."

"Oh, I think you do," insisted Howison. "The other night in town you made quite a point of how you stood behind your crew, regardless. What they were responsible for, you were responsible for. That's what you said, Ben. I'm just taking you at your word. It's like this. Somebody in your outfit slow-elked a critter of mine, and I've come after one of yours in return. That make things plain enough?"

Walrode's glance tightened still more and a corner of his mouth curled in mocking retort.

"You know, Howison, I used to think you were reasonably smart. You're not. You're plain stupid if you think you can pin anything like that on this outfit. Try telling it to Miles Sulivane or Jock Dunaway or Henry Kleyburg. They'd laugh at you, just like they did the other night."

"Maybe," conceded Howison briefly. "But I'm not laughing, which you'd better believe. Could be, you know, the others were so busy laughing they didn't spot the lie that I did. I rode in here to make sure you knew what I'm about to do and why I'm doing it. I'm collecting a Sawbuck two year old on my way home, Ben. Now you have it!"

His mouth as ugly and heavy as Howison had ever seen it, Ben Walrode turned his head and called harsh order.

"Chirk, if he tries to ride out before I say he can, shoot that buckskin right out from under him!"

Howison came up straight in his saddle, glance swinging. Yonder, in the doorway of the combined cookshack and bunkhouse, a Winchester ready in his hands, stood Chirk Dennis. The marks of the going over he had taken from Tap Geer were dark stains on his bruised and swollen face, and the look he fixed on Howison was hungry and wicked. Hip high and level, the gun he held laid out its steady threat.

Howison brought his glance back to Walrode. "Take it easy, Ben. Don't get so far out on a limb you can't back off it. Don't start something you can't stop. Tell your man to put that rifle away before he gets it fed to him, a foot at a time!"

The remark set Chirk Dennis off. He came away from the cookshack at a clumsy, plunging, heavy-legged run, rifle pushing its threat even more openly.

"Try it!" he shrilled savagely. "Go ahead, try it! You and that friend of yours — Geer — throwin' your weight around . . . ! Yeah, go ahead and try it!"

On leaving home, Howison had considered taking a gun along, then decided against it. Even while disliking Ben Walrode intensely, and trusting him not at all, he still hoped that sound reasoning might still be arrived at and some sort of peaceful accord be established without need of deepening violence. Such had been his thought and intent, but here was stark evidence that he had been wrong.

Again he put his glance on Walrode, who, along with Jack Labine and Nick Bodie, had moved in closer.

"Ben, I've said what I came to say. Now I'm riding out. If Dennis uses that gun to stop me, he'll be setting off something all of you'll come to wish he hadn't!"

"Big talk!" jeered Walrode. "Just big talk!" He came another quick stride ahead and grabbed the buckskin's rein. "All right, boys! Haul him out of that saddle and work him down to size!"

They started for him, Labine and Bodie, one on either side. Stung with the dismal knowledge that he was surely in for it, Howison made the most of a temporary advantage of position. He slid his feet from the stirrups and as Bodie came in on his right, reaching for him, he drove a solid toe into Bodie's chest, knocking him backward. Then, on the other side, he dove headlong at Jack Labine.

He got a shoulder into the Sawbuck foreman and rode him down. The force of his lunge carried him on and over, and his head rammed the hard earth, the impact dazing him. By the time he recovered and gained his feet, Jack Labine was also up and coming at him. Labine's arms were long, his fists bony and hard. Twice they reached and punished Howison before he could set himself and put over a slashing blow of his own.

When he did, it was a good one, making a mess of Labine's mouth, driving him back and bringing a gush of crimson from mashed lips. Howison kept after him, nailing him with a short, driving hook to the side of the neck that made Labine sag and wobble. But then it was Nick Bodie, circling the lunging, rearing buckskin, who came up from behind and slugged Howison viciously at the base of the skull, a numbing blow that drove him forward to his knees. He was that way, wide open and unable to protect himself, when Jack Labine stepped in and clubbed him savagely on the jaw.

The world turning dim, Howison went all the way down. Boots slammed into him again and again, and under this punishment, the stricken numbness washed all through him and consciousness became just a thin and straining thread.

The shout, when it came, seemed to arrive from some great distance. But it was charged with outrage, and on the heels of it the drive of the merciless boots ceased and someone had hold of him, lifting him to a sitting position. The arm steadying him was strong, and the voice, sounding again, deep and harshly growling, belonged to Henry Kleyburg.

"Ben, what is this? What were you trying to do, have this man kicked to death?"

With the punishment stopped, the numbness fading, and the world returning to full focus, Dave Howison stumbled to his feet, humped over from the pain in his boot-punished ribs. He blinked his eyes, scrubbed a hand across his face, and managed a strained, crooked grin as he made mumbled comment.

"Ben's idea of a little fun, Henry. Great guy, Ben. You know — upright and big-hearted. Only, he sure likes the odds on his side. Give me time to straighten out a little, and I'll take on the brave lads in separate chunks. You know, Henry, one at a time. That includes Ben — noble old Ben . . . !"

He laughed then, but it wasn't a good sound, as he was near to retching because of the cold fury that convulsed him.

Standing beside him, Henry Kleyburg repeated his growling demand. "What's the answer to this, Ben?"

Startled as he had been by Howison's

appearance, Ben Walrode was caught even more off balance when Henry Kleyburg and Milt Shannon came whirling up in Kleyburg's buckboard. And Kleyburg's reaction had been equally disconcerting. Riding the brake hard, the cattleman had brought his rig to a wheel-skidding halt and was out of it in a single leap. He had charged into Jack Labine and Nick Bodie, driving them aside and standing over Howison protectively. Now, stern and accusing, he was demanding an answer not easy to arrive at.

Shrugging sullenly, Walrode gave the first that came to mind. "He rode in here, asking for trouble. He found it."

Henry Kleyburg looked around, getting a second and clearer picture of the setup. There was Chirk Dennis, ready Winchester still in his hands. There were Jack Labine and Nick Bodie, Labine with pouted, bloody lips, and Nick Bodie with a glance that was dark and hating. Finally, there was Ben Walrode, still gripping the buckskin's rein, his eyes surly, his mouth in its heavy, brutal set. Reproof filled Kleyburg's glance and his retort was blunt.

"Won't do, Ben. More behind this than that — a lot more." He turned to Howison. "What's your side, Dave?"

Howison had both hands pressed hard against his body and he spoke slowly between grimaces of pain.

"I came to tell Walrode I was collecting a Sawbuck beef critter for the one of mine his men slow-elked. He gave me the big laugh and told Dennis to shoot the buckskin out from under me if I tried to leave. Then he turned Labine and Bodie loose, with orders to do a good job on me. I don't know how good it would have been or how long it would have lasted if you hadn't come along. Now, like I said, we'll see about these brave buckos, when they got to dance, one at a time." He looked at Labine, moved a step that way. "Come and get it, Jack. When I'm done with you I'll make Bodie beg like a dog. And finally, we'll have a look at the real color of Ben's spine. Which is something I've long wondered about."

Henry Kleyburg caught him by the arm. "That won't do, either." Angry exasperation rumbled out of the cattleman. "Damn this business of always having to quiet you people down! Dave, I'm getting rid of you again. Go some place and cool off."

Milt Shannon, who had picked up the reins and quieted the buckboard team when Henry Kleyburg jumped to

Howison's aid, now made pronouncement of his own.

"Dave, you do as Henry says. Dennis, put that Winchester away before I come and take it away. And Ben — when Henry gets through with you, I got a few things for your ears."

The veiled sullenness in Ben Walrode deepened, but Howison, eyeing Kleyburg and Shannon with speculative surprise, managed a thin, wry smile.

"Maybe I had better get along at that, much as I'd like to stick around and listen. I've a feeling things could be interesting."

He took over the buckskin's rein, his glance raking Walrode with a flat and now deathless enmity.

"One fine day it's going to be just you and me, Ben. That you can count on. Yeah, just you and me. Then we'll see! Now, once more I say it — on the way home I'm picking up the critter you owe me. You won't need to vent the brand; I'll take care of that."

He went into his saddle with a slow, jaw-tightening effort. He swung the horse and headed away. Still edgy with excitement, the buckskin wanted to run, but he held it to a swinging canter that was easier on his punished ribs.

Henry Kleyburg watched him go before turning to Walrode accusingly.

"Ben, I'm ashamed of you. Two, three to one, and one of you with a gun. And you standing by to allow it, even ordering it."

A flare showed in Walrode's pale eyes. "Don't you start rawhiding me, Henry. I'm not about to take it from you or anybody else. It's like I say. Howison rode in here looking for trouble. He found it."

"A man," said Kleyburg sternly, "would have to come at me pretty strong before I'd order a rider of mine to wave a gun at him. Dave Howison was unarmed, so how do you justify yourself?"

"I don't have to," Walrode retorted. "You heard Howison throw some tough talk at me in the meeting the other night. He did the same to Jack Labine. Now he rides in here with still more of it, and I just wasn't going to swallow it. This was my way of shutting him up. It suits me. I don't care if it doesn't suit anybody else."

Kleyburg studied him for a moment, then turned away. He climbed into the buckboard and retrieved the reins from Milt Shannon, after which he put his glance on Walrode again.

"No need to ask any more questions, I see. You know, Ben, my women folks are

134

pretty shrewd people, much more so than I've been. Oh, Sue was set to give you the benefit of the doubt until she rode out that trail with Dave Howison yesterday. But last night she had to admit that her mother and Howison have been right about you all along. I was the really blind one. But no more! You can leave me out of that association idea of yours. I want no part of it!"

A slight break showed in Walrode's hostile front. "You and me, Henry," he said placatingly — "we got no quarrel. Along with Miles Sulivane and Jock Dunaway we can . . ."

"No!" cut in Kleyburg, growling. "I'm out. But there is one thing I'd like to know. Just what you figured to gain in planting slow-elked meat on Price Tedrow? Or maybe you don't want to answer up to that."

The lines about Walrode's mouth pulled deeper and uglier and the wall of sullenness became solid again.

"If you're willing to believe that, to take the word of a nester and side with him against people of your own kind, then maybe it's just as well you do pull out on Miles and Jock and me."

"I'm not siding for or against anyone," returned Kleyburg with stern finality. "All

135

I'm interested in is the truth. And I do not find it here."

He would have hauled the team around, but Milt Shannon made him hold up a moment longer.

"Ben," said the sheriff, "I'm not going to need any help in running my office. Not from you or anybody else. Any premises that need searching for any reason, I'll handle the chore alone. Also and besides, there'll be no more long riding and pushing weaker folks around, nester or no. You hear me, Ben? And you, Labine? I'm the elected law in Jubilee Basin and from now on, everybody best remember it so. All right, Henry — let's get back to town."

They drove away, leaving behind them a tense, surly silence. Ben Walrode stared after the departing buckboard, heavy lips pulling and twisting, pale eyes congested with a seething inner turbulence. Labine and Bodie and Dennis watched him, waiting. Finally Labine spoke.

"That does it, Ben. The lid's off. And we've shown too much of our hand to stop half way. Either we put in all our chips and hit for the whole pot, or we get out of the game completely. What's it to be — yes, or no?"

Walrode rose on his toes, filled his chest

as though making ready for some kind of explosive effort. When his answer came it was thick and harsh.

"It's yes, of course. Saddle up and go locate Jett Chesbro. Tell him we're ready to do business, starting tonight!"

CHAPTER

VII

Heading away from Sawbuck headquarters, Dave Howison held to the south bank of Big Stony Creek as far as the main basin road, thereafter crossing Big Stony by way of the bridge below town and moving on into Basin City. Holding the buckskin to a walk as he traveled the street's length, his searching glance presently located the very person he was hoping to see.

Tap Geer occupied a favorite chair beside the door of the Trading Post. Leaning against the wall beside him, Luke Casper was a short, wide figure in the usual flour-dusted blue-denim apron. The pair of them watched with casual interest until Howison hauled up at the hitch rail and dismounted with a slow, stiffened care. Whereupon, quickening concern moved Tap to speech.

"Last time I saw him, Luke, he was on the sunny side of thirty. But now he acts like he was a hundred years old."

Howison grinned twistedly as he climbed the platform steps. "And feel it," he said. "Cast your eyes, gentlemen, on the frayed out result of a very rough morning."

Tap's interest deepened. "Don't tell me the buckskin caught you looking the other way and kicked you out of the corral? I thought you'd gentled the brute better than that."

Howison pulled up a second chair and sank into it with a grunt of relief. "I got kicked, all right," he admitted. "But not by a horse." He passed a hand carefully across his face. "I also got belted a couple of good ones in the mug. Altogether, I repeat, a rough, rough morning."

By this time Tap was on the edge of his chair, eaten with curiosity. "All right — all right," he urged impatiently. "Let's have it. What happened?"

Howison told it, as matter-of-fact and objective as sore ribs and a couched, still-simmering anger would allow.

"They'd have done me up in real style if Henry Kleyburg and Milt Shannon hadn't come along. Kleyburg hauled Labine and Bodie off, while Shannon told Chirk Dennis what for about the rifle. All in all, I'd guess the appearance of Henry and Milt — along with their attitudes — sort of jolted Ben and his crowd."

"Where's your good sense?" railed Tap heatedly. "After telling off Walrode and Labine the way you have, you should have known better than ride into such a spot without a gun on you. What with this and that beginning to blow across the range, you better turn smart, my friend."

Howison brooded, grave faced, while he twisted up a cigarette. "Maybe I will," he nodded slowly. "Still and all, the last thing any of us want to see is a smoke rolling. There should be some saner way to settle matters."

"Sure there should," agreed Tap vehemently. "Only there ain't — not with Ben Walrode settin' up deadlines and tryin' to push everybody around."

"Which reminds me," Howison said with a glint of humor. "You sure must have stomped all over Chirk Dennis. Most wore your fists out on him, didn't you? And maybe an ax handle or two? He sure looked like you did. He was black and blue and swelled all out of shape. What are you, half man, half tiger?"

"Pure wildcat," grunted Luke Casper. "Thinks he is, anyhow."

Tap grinned. "Guess I was a little rough. I'd been sittin' here, feelin' some mean and snappy when Dennis showed up. I figured it was a good time to let the Sawbuck crowd know they couldn't push me around."

"Don't let it make you too proud," Howison said, turning serious. "I just found out that Ben and his boys can be pretty mean hombres. Much as we might like to take a cut at them, we'll be smart to sit tight a little longer until they show more of their hand. In the meantime, you keep out of their way."

Luke Casper, who had been listening quietly, cleared his throat and spoke some troubled thoughts. "Dave, you seem pretty positive that Sawbuck slow-elked that beef critter of yours and planted the meat on Price Tedrow. Why would they do that? What could Ben Walrode hope to gain by it? There's something that has me fighting my head. I can't figure it."

"I see it this way, Luke," said Howison soberly. "Ben's call for a protective association is based on his contention that rustling is going on. Not all of us are convinced this is so, not to the extent of justifying the end Ben is calling for. Which Ben knows, so he had this slow-elking deal pulled just before the meeting the other night as an angle to push his idea along. He was gambling, of course, that with the accepted feeling of distrust toward any and all nesters, everybody would believe Tedrow guilty as charged and just another liar should he claim otherwise."

"I can savvy that, all right," Casper nodded. "But now we come up against the fact that rustling is, or is not, going on. And if it isn't, what's Ben's point in claiming it is?"

"There," said Howison meaningly, "is the joker in the deck."

"How so?" demanded Casper.

"Like this," Howison told him. "Couple of seasons back, Woody Biggs and I drove a small shipping herd to Winnemucca. There was a medicine show in town. Running it was the usual fakir. You know the kind — a fast talker who picked cards out of the air and rabbits out of a hat. He was pretty good at it, too, and sure had some Basque sheepherders wide-eyed and open-mouthed. He might even have fooled me some. But not old Woody. His whole deal, Woody said, was to keep people watching one hand while he did monkey business with the other. That give you some idea?"

Luke wagged his head up and down. "If you don't want people to watch you, you keep them watching someone else. That it?"

"Part of it. The rest is — who's going to figure you a thief in the night, if you ride as a staunch defender of the law by day?"

Howison left it so, grunting and sweating as he got to his feet.

"You," declared Tap pointedly, "better go see Doc Church about those ribs."

Howison shook his head. "They'll loosen up if I keep on the move. And you remember what I said about staying out of trouble."

Once beyond town, Howison cut away toward the sprawling lower slopes of Chancellor Peak, remembering the scatter of Sawbuck stock he had stirred up in the willow swamp along Big Stony. He had made his brag about taking home one of them, and he had to make it good.

Back at the Trading Post, Luke Casper voiced sober conclusion. "Everything boiled down, it seems Dave figures Ben Walrode up to some pretty shady business. Much as I like Dave, and knowing how highhanded Ben can be in some ways, I still find it hard to believe he would step completely across the line and help himself to anything that wasn't truly his."

"Different here!" exclaimed Tap strongly. "I wouldn't put anything past

Ben Walrode. He's already spread himself over a big chunk of government range south of Big Stony and now sets up a deadline to keep other folks off it. If that ain't helpin' yourself to what ain't yours, then I don't know what is."

"Deadline just for you, Tap," reminded Casper dryly.

"So far, yeah," Tap admitted. "But if he can make it stick, then pretty soon it becomes a deadline for everybody. And who knows what kind of shady business could go on behind it? I string along with Dave Howison. He don't fool easy, and if he says Ben Walrode has the makings of a crook, that's good enough for me."

"You're spoiling my day," growled Luke. So saying, he turned back into the store.

Left alone and stirred by the word Dave Howison had left with him, Tap Geer grew restless. Along with an insouciant approach to life, Tap owned a lively imagination that now was envisioning all manner of future possibilities, some of them ominous. One thing was very certain. In turning his men loose on Howison, Ben Walrode had started something that would not go unanswered. For while Dave Howison was normally a well balanced, fairly even-tempered individual, Tap knew it was the quiet sort who became the real curly wolves, once you got them stirred up. Every Sawbuck hand who mixed in on that gang attack sooner or later would pay for their fun, and big! Including Ben Walrode.

Tap had located a forgotten, half-empty sack of Durham in one of his saddlebags, so now he built a thin cigarette and sucked at it with miserly care while his rampaging thoughts took him further and further, the bite of excitement deepening. What was it Woody Biggs figured the medicine man did? Kept you watching one hand while doing monkey business with the other!

Something of the sort, Dave Howison had declared, could have been Ben Walrode's original plan, and why he had tried to frame a slow-elking charge on Price Tedrow. But that hadn't worked out the way Ben expected, so now he had moved more into the open. In making that attack on Dave Howison he had started something he would have to see to a finish, regardless of what that finish toted up to. It wasn't a thing you could back away from, with everybody willing to forgive and forget. Had it been a few punches swapped in a fair, stand-up argument between two men, it might in time be glossed over. But a gang attack, backed by the threat of a gun, was another affair entirely. Arrogant and domineering as he was, Ben Walrode must have been aware of this. Which meant that whatever he had in mind, he was now fully committed to, with no place to go but right on down the trail he had chosen.

Where did that trail lead? What lay at the end of it?

Tap chased these two questions back and forth through coiling cigarette smoke and came up with the inevitable conclusions. If you wanted to find something, you went looking for it. If you hoped to find out what kind of monkey business might be going on south of Big Stony, that's where you had to go, deadline or no deadline.

Decision solidly arrived at, Tap dredged the last atom of satisfaction from his cigarette, discarded the butt, and headed for Barney Tuttle's cabin and the rickety corral behind it, where he kept his horse. Half an hour later he was gone from town, a meager outfit tied behind his saddle and his rifle slung under his leg. He told no one where he was going or what he was about, but it never hurt to cover your trail. So he rode due west toward Cold River and the rim beyond.

In time, this direction brought him on to

Claymore range, where Jock Dunaway and his Shoshone Indian rider, Joe Ruiz, were branding and earmarking some calves along one of the river flats. Old Jock was tending the fire and the iron, while Ruiz did the roping and heavy muscle work. When Tap rode up, Ruiz had a husky little bull calf bucking and fighting at the end of his rope, and when Ruiz left his saddle to flank the little brute, he found himself with a handful of trouble. Tap swung down immediately and gave a hand. Between them they quickly flattened and stretched the calf. Joe Ruiz grinned his sweating thanks.

Tap wasn't too sure how Jock Dunaway would feel about his presence, but faced him cheerfully as the stocky, red-faced old Scotchman came up with the iron.

"You got a good critter there, Jock. Make you some money a couple of years from now."

Old Jock only grunted in reply. He set the iron and the smoke curled up, rank with the stench of singed hair and scorched hide. The calf bawled its pain and fright and a belligerent cow advanced in threat. Tap waved his hat in her face, headed her off. Jock Dunaway tossed the iron aside to cool and earmarked the calf, which, when then freed, went away in a bouncing rush, seeking mother comfort. Dunaway stamped out the fire and called to Ruiz.

"That's the last one, Joe. Now let's push everything down river a bit."

Tap looked around, wondering about this. "Still plenty of good grass here, Jock."

Dunaway got out his pipe, packed it with calloused fingers.

" 'Tis because of Sulivane," he explained gruffly. "An animal of mine gets across his line for a mouthful of grass, I hear about it. As he would tell it, everybody is out to rob Miles Sulivane." He peered at Tap out of pinched, aging eyes that showed the barest hint of a twinkle. "Now I've seen a cow thief or two in my time, but I must say you do not have the look of such about you."

"Well now — thanks!" exclaimed the startled and gratified Tap. "Sure glad to hear you say that, Jock. Miles Sulivane and some others might not agree with you."

Old Jock nodded, running a blazing sulphur match back and forth across the deeply charred bowl of his pipe, his weather-ruddied cheeks caving inward as he puffed. He snuffed out the match and tossed it into the blackened fire embers.

"A contentious one, Sulivane — and suspicious of all. Were I a younger man, no doubt we might argue, he and I. But my years keep me seeking peace — up to a limit. Past that — well . . . !" The old fellow shrugged, his glance searching Tap again. " 'Tis a fine thing to be young, laddie, with the world full of the fun and freedom of chasin' your shadow here and yon. But see to it that you dinna' waste too many of the good years. Somewhere along the way, every man must set his spurs into a real and solid purpose."

Tap hung on for a little time, helping Dunaway and Joe Ruiz chouse cattle out of the willows and start them moving downstream — after which he sought a shallows and sent his horse splashing across the river. Here the rim towered immediately above him, its dark lava face stark and frowning in the flare of the sun. At first glance, it seemed an almost unscalable barrier, but Tap skirted confidently along the base of it, dodging the fanned-out edges of tallus slides, threading thickets of mountain mahogany, and crossing stretches of flinty, hostile ground where scanty sagebrush and stunted junipers struggled for a foothold. In time, he struck a well-marked trail.

This angled up the rim in long, steep-slanted switchbacks. Here the sun struck warmly, and Tap rode slack and easy, letting his hard-working horse pause when it wished for a breather. At such times, he twisted in his saddle to look back at the widespread distances of the flats below, and his thoughts grew sober.

This was a good land, to him the best of lands, and he knew it well. Big as it was and as far reaching in its limits, it held few trails that did not skirt the burned-out ashes of his many campfires or bear some sign of his carefree wanderings. No man could live as close to any land as Tap had to this one, and to know its many flavors and its beckoning freedoms, without achieving a deep and abiding affinity for it. Nor could he face the prospect of having to leave it, uncaring or without concern. Just the thought of such a possibility brought Tap up straight in staunch and defiant rejection.

No, by God! And to hell with Ben Walrode . . . !

Cresting the rim, the trail led immediately into timber, pine and fir, with here and there a stand of silver-barked, golden-leafed aspens. Here morning's breath lingered to sweeten the world and under the touch of it, Tap's mood brightened and moved him to a cheerful whistling. He was still warbling when he broke into an extensive, high country meadow that held a reed-fringed, spring-fed lake. All around white-faced cattle were in evidence, and at the far end of the clearing the chimney of a log-built cabin gave off a thin drift of fat pine-wood smoke to spice the air.

When Tap rode up, Pete Mallory appeared in the cabin doorway, looking sleepy and disheveled. Along with the scent of wood smoke, Tap now caught the flavor of coffee. This he sniffed appreciatively and spoke at large.

"Man must be a lazy son-of-a-gun to be still wrastlin' with breakfast when morning's near run out."

Pete Mallory yawned. "Heck with you, Mister Geer! For your information I got darn little sleep last night, what with havin' to lend a helpin' hand to a cow in some trouble, tryin' to drop her calf. Now there could be some who wouldn't be bothered about such things. But me, I'm a poor man, so a cow is a cow and a calf is a calf, and I can't afford riskin' the loss of nary one of them. Also and besides, if you don't like my idea of cookin' up a late breakfast, what you sniffin' so eager about?"

"Can I help it if any coffee is good coffee to me, any old time?"

Tap was so plaintive about this, Pete had

to grin as he waved an inviting hand. "Light down, boy, and dig in."

"What," he asked, a little later, "brings you drifting around up here?"

"Maybe to see if you were still healthy and able," Tap suggested.

Pete grunted skeptically. "Any reason why I shouldn't be?"

Tap shrugged. "What with deadlines being laid down and innocent nesters framed for slow-elking, I just wondered."

"You don't have to wonder about me," vowed Pete. "I had my say about that kind of business the other night in town. Handed it right into friend Walrode's teeth, I did. Told him if he or any of his crowd tried to push me around, somebody would get shot. And it wouldn't be me!"

"Ben don't learn easy and can get rough, real rough," warned Tap, then telling about Dave Howison's misadventure at Sawbuck. "Dave said they'd have kicked in his ribs for sure if Henry Kleyburg and Milt Shannon hadn't happened along. Pete, this thing could get bad, real bad. Ben Walrode is cooking up some kind of deal he intends to go through with, come hell or high water. I'm wondering what it could be."

Pete scowled and scratched his head in thought. "Might pay a man to ride the back trails and do some watchin' and listenin'.""

"Just where I'm heading now," Tap admitted. "And you do some of that watching and listening. Should you run across something, get the word to Dave Howison. He's the one who has his eyes real wide open."

"That I'll do," promised Pete. "I'll mosey around."

Fortified with hot coffee, Tap went on his way, and in time reached the edge of the steep-walled, rock-ribbed lateral defile through the black lava mass of Cold River Rim that was Horsehead Canyon. Hauled up here on a craggy point, he looked over what he could see of the winding run of the canyon road. On one stretch near the upper end a double hitch freight outfit behind a toiling string of mules crawled slowly toward eventual destination of Basin City. Carrying faintly up through the canyon's warm stillness came the measured, chiming cadence of the hame bells of the team leaders.

Waiting until the freight outfit had moved beyond sight around another turn, and satisfied that the rest of the canyon was empty, Tap worked his way down, cleared the road, made steep drop-off to a river crossing, then climbed the far side of the canyon and moved on into the wild, ruggedly hostile lava badlands beyond. Outlaw country, this, Tap thought, full of brush shrouded potholes, jagged, sprawling ridges, and furtive, tangled trails for furtive men to ride.

Jett Chesbro country.

Since his meeting with that outlaw and the consequent uproar that came of it, Tap had done considerable thinking about the man. He had seen Chesbro on but few occasions and spoken to him only once, which was on the day he shared coffee with him. That Chesbro probably deserved the shady reputation basin opinion accorded him, Tap was willing to concede. Still and all, Chesbro had never done him any wrong and until he did, Tap vowed, he would accept the man at his face value. And to hell with Jubilee Basin opinion, generated for the most part by Ben Walrode. Right now, as Tap saw it, Ben Walrode offered far more cause for worry than Jett Chesbro ever had.

Several times in the past, Tap had skirted the edge of these badlands, but had never moved into them as deeply as now. The farther he went, the more he had to admit that if a rustler wanted the right kind of country to operate his special business in, he couldn't do better than this.

Once he knew this country well, a man might move a sizable herd of rustled stock into it, break the herd up into small bunches, and scatter them in such a way it would take a virtual army of men to recover even the smallest part of them. Later, when the pressure of pursuit was off, the cattle could be moved on into some far southern range and disposed of there. Yes, sir, this country was made to order for something like that.

Tap struck faint trails, followed them and ran into other traces that in turn became lost in myriad twists and turnings. To hold to a reasonably straight line was impossible, so broken and scattered were the harsh-spined lava ridges that lifted to bar the way, so narrow and twisted the gulches and brush-clotted potholes between them.

What he was searching for just now was a suitable spot to throw off his saddle and make camp. He came across several water holes, with plenty of sign of wildlife about them, but he had to find a camp where more than water was available, where there would be some forage for his horse.

In time he came to it, a small, lava-ringed flat that held a fair spread of grass as well as water. Here he startled a couple of beef cattle that left in a pounding rush, wild as deer — a pair of strays, now running free, and intent on staying so.

By the time he had his meager camp set up, the sun was well in the west and hunger was stirring in him. He put together a fire of dry mahogany brush that would give off little smoke, and cooked and ate his frugal meal. Then he twisted up a cigarette and took stock. He now was well south of that deadline Ben Walrode had set up, but to hell with Walrode! He would, Tap decided grimly, prowl this country and all the range between it and Big Stony Creek until he got some idea of what Ben Walrode was up to.

Cigarette smoked out, stomach full, soul at peace for the moment at least, Tap lay back to watch full night settle in and the stars come out. This he liked, a lonely camp where a man might sense the world's freedom at its fullest and reduce life to its simplest essentials.

For a time, he kept his fire going, burning small and ruddy, for firelight had a way of tying a man to security. But at length it shrank to fading coals, then gray ash; the dark closed in and only the light of the stars remained. Tap took off his boots, rolled in his blanket, and found deep sleep close to the earth.

From the eminence of one of the two raw-hide-backed chairs on the porch of the Bar 88 ranch house, Dave Howison moodily watched the afternoon hours slip away across the basin miles. He was a man sore in mind and spirit as well as in body. The estimate of the extent of his physical miseries as he had explained them to Tap Geer and Luke Casper had proved decidedly faulty; riding had done anything but ease the condition of his punished ribs.

On arrival at the home ranch, it had taken grim, teeth-gritting effort to leave his saddle, and he was more than willing to let Woody Biggs take care of the Sawbuck steer he had picked up along Big Stony. Woody quickly corralled the animal, then returned full of concern, questions, and copious scoldings.

He herded Howison into the ranch-house kitchen, set out an old galvanized washtub, and made Howison strip and squat in it. Then he poured in the hot water and more hot water until Howison swore mightily, vowing he was being boiled alive. Woody swore right back and added more hot water, filling the tub to the brim.

It was, of course, exactly what was needed, and when Howison finally emerged, turkey red to his armpits, he was able to straighten up and take reasonably deep breaths without grunting with pain. He felt halfway human again, though quite content to seek the comfort of his chair.

There was, however, no comfort in his thoughts. He owned his share of strong pride and self-respect, and there had been little of either showing in the situation Henry Kleyburg and Milt Shannon had witnessed at Sawbuck, with him flat on the ground getting kicked like a whipped dog.

True, when back on his feet, he had challenged Ben Walrode and the Sawbuck crew to make another try, man to man, but nothing came of that. Or could have, at the time. It had been just an outpouring of words that proved nothing except that he was convulsed with bleak fury, an anger that would never be fully cooled until he had made the words good at some future time and place.

Just thinking about it freshened the inner

fire and made him squirm restlessly, which move brought immediate protest from the bruised ribs, and he swore over this, fretful with frustration. Quickly after, he went quite still, his glance fixed on the lower ford of Bannock Creek, where Sue Kleyburg, up on her little pinto pony, splashed across and came upslope to the house.

Howison watched her approach with a grave intentness. As always, the sight of this girl pleased him. One who carried herself with natural grace, in or out of the saddle, she was slim, spirited, and competent, with a mind of her own and a willingness to speak it. Also, she owned a complete honesty, ever reflected by the directness of her blue-eyed glance. She was, and would always be, Howison mused, a difficult person to lie to.

This vagrant thought quirked his lips with a touch of amusement that was still in evidence when the girl swung from her saddle and stepped up on the porch, slapping a pair of gauntlet gloves against the sweep of her divided skirt. Her quick, direct glance did not miss Howison's expression, and she questioned it tartly.

"Something amuses you?"

"Nothing of the sort," denied Howison

quickly. "I'm just happy, that's all. I'm always happy when you're around. Haul up that other chair. Sit by me, and let me feast my eyes on beauty."

Sue sniffed. "Now you're turning sneaky. I can always tell. When you start spreading the blarney, it's sure sign you're about to speak with a forked tongue. Well, Mister Howison, it will do you no good to try and feed me fairy tales, as I happen to know all about what happened at Sawbuck." She squared the other chair around, settled into it, and viewed him critically. "You show the signs of wear and tear."

"And feel the effects of same," he admitted dryly. "Your dad and Milt Shannon sure showed up at the right time. Right about then I wasn't doing much good for myself, while Ben Walrode was enjoying every minute of it. It could have been worthwhile, though, as I've a feeling Henry Kleyburg finally got a real, clear look at good old Ben."

Sue nodded soberly. "He did, and is all upset. Poor Dad — you know how he is. So direct and straightforward. With him, it is day or night, black or white, right or wrong. Nothing half way. When he believes in anything, he believes fully, and when it comes to pieces about his ears, it sets him off. He has Mother and me really worried this time."

Howison cocked a concerned eye. "How so?"

"Well, once he's convinced something is wrong, he can't rest until he's had his try at making it right."

"Which in this case would be Ben Walrode and what he's really up to?"

Sue nodded again and spoke with a rush of feeling. "Can't this affair between you and Ben be settled without the sort of thing that happened at Sawbuck? Or perhaps something even worse? Can't it be quieted down before everybody gets involved? Oh, I'm not blaming you, Dave. Only, you know . . ."

"Yeah," he said gently, "I know."

His grave glance reached out to mark the run of afternoon shadow sifting through the willows along the creek. There could be no doubting this girl's real concern. But there was nothing he could say to lessen it, not while speaking the truth. Because he knew how he felt and, just as certainly, how Ben Walrode felt. It added up to a bitter, no-quarter showdown, regardless of the cost. He stirred and brought his glance back to her.

"Yeah," he repeated, "I know how it is.

Certainly I'd like to see the range kept quiet and peaceful. But there's Ben and there's me, and it shapes up that one or the other of us has to go, if not in this squaring off, then at some future one. The more I think about it, the more I feel it was written in the book a long time ago. Right now Ben has some kind of knot in that bullet head of his that is eating him up. For one thing, he's the sort who has to be top dog, no matter what he has to do to get there. And you don't stop a man like that with soft words. If you try, he'll figure you weak and afraid. You have to use something weightier and more final, like a — well — like a . . . !"

He did not finish the thought, but Sue, understanding fully, did so in a small, tight voice. "Like a gun?"

Howison nodded. "It's an ugly prospect that I certainly don't care for, but I can't afford to turn my back on it. Also, as it lies mainly between Ben and me, I'd like to keep it so, with no one else involved. However, knowing the kind of man Henry Kleyburg is, I don't see him staying wholly neutral, particularly since he's now had his good look at Walrode with the mask off. Wish I could tell you something different, Sue, but I know you'd never settle for anything but the truth."

Her head tipped slowly up and down, and the westering sun, slanting in under the porch overhang, picked up warm glints in her hair. She looked at Howison in sober appraisal.

"When it comes to issues, no one can move you a single step. They might beat you within an inch of your life, but they will never change you. Right now, though black and blue from your last affair, you're figuring how you'll handle the next meeting."

Howison's lips quirked. "You make me out a regular hell bender, when I'm really a timid soul."

Sue scoffed. "You're a tough, determined brute, that's what you are. Besides being stubborn, contrary, and exasperating!"

From the open doorway, Woody Biggs applauded vigorously. "That's the stuff, Susie! Lay on the rawhide. He's got it coming. And, long as you're here, you best stay for supper. I just put a raisin pie in the oven."

Woody was in his undershirt, sleeves rolled to a pair of bony elbows. A flour-sack apron sagged at his gaunt middle, and he was scrubbed until his weathered cheeks showed pink through a fringe of grizzled whiskers. Under shaggy brows his eyes were magpie bright.

Sue exclaimed, "Supper? Oh, Woody — I'm not sure that I can."

"Of course you can," put in Howison quickly. "Consider it settled. Later, I'll squire you home."

"You will not! You're in no condition to ride. You'd break in half."

Howison's faint grin showed again. "I'll risk it for the chance to ride with you."

Sue got to her feet. "Did I say stubborn! Woody, if I'm to help eat that pie, I intend to earn it. I'll set the table."

"And in the meantime," Howison called after her, "how about another truce?"

She paused in the doorway, looking back at him. For all her fiery, spirited moods, ever evident was that basic sweetness of complete honesty.

"Truce it is," she nodded. "Which will make supper taste better."

What with the hot-water treatment Woody Biggs had given him, plus several hours of rest, and now further bolstered by a good meal, Howison was able to sit his saddle again without too much discomfort. He spoke cheerfully as he and Sue Kleyburg jogged off through the cooling, smoke-blue tide of dusk.

"Susie, in case you don't realize it, this is saving my life. Bless you for stopping by to stir me up."

"I didn't stop by to stir you up," came the tart retort. "My hope was to calm you down and keep you from tearing around breathing fire and fury and getting into more trouble."

"You do me wrong," Howison stated. "I'm no trouble hunter and you know it."

Silent for a moment, Sue sighed. "I guess I do. Mother has a saying about men shaping events and events shaping men, with nothing much a body can do about it but choose a side and hope for the best."

"Just so," murmured Howison. "Which side are you on, Susie?"

Again she was slow in answering. When she did her words were subdued. "I just ate supper with you, didn't I?"

She flicked the pinto with the rein ends, lifting it to a run. Howison did not try and keep pace and presently, a little farther along the way, she pulled up waiting for him.

"Sorry," she said contritely. "I didn't mean to run away from you. But you always — well — talk me into such a corner."

Howison chuckled. "Won't say another word without your permission."

She held him to his word, and the balance of the ride was a silent one. But it was a good silence because it held an understanding between these two people. They watched the full dark come down and the stars wink out and throw down their brilliance. A small drift of vagrant wind, scuttling across the world, brushed by and was gone. The pure, cool call of a night hawk sifted out of the star-clustered sky, and there was, thought Howison, something vital even in the dust that lifted from the trail. The horses sensed the mood of the moment and moved with a slacked ease.

In time, lights beckoned, and from the deep gallery of the ranch house ahead came Henry Kleyburg's rumbling growl in mild reproof. "Daughter, you should let us know when you expect to be this late. Time was when I wouldn't have worried, but the way things are shaping up now . . . !"

"Blame me, Woody Biggs, and a raisin pie, Henry," explained Howison quickly. "We kept Sue to supper."

Mrs. Kleyburg, who had been sitting with her husband, spoke her gentle relief. "Woody and his raisin pies. They'd lure a king off his throne. Wish I'd been there, David."

Henry Kleyburg moved up to take over

Sue's horse. Swinging lithely down, Sue gave him a quick peck on the cheek.

"Sorry, Dad. But you mustn't worry about me. I'm a big girl now." She started away, then paused. "Thanks for seeing me home, David. You can be rather nice, when you try."

She went on, and her father, staring after her through the dark, murmured gruffly, "The same today as way back when she was just a little twig. Independent as a jay bird on a high limb." He looked up at Howison. "Didn't expect to see you in a saddle so soon after that mess at Sawbuck. Come along. I got things to say."

Howison followed over to the corrals. While stripping headstall and saddle off the pinto, Kleyburg made blunt demand. "Dave, where's this thing to stop? I don't like what I see between you and Walrode. I don't like it a bit!"

Howison slouched in his saddle, twisting up a cigarette purely by feel. "I know," he agreed. "Just the same, it has to be faced. One thing I want understood, Henry. It's strictly between Ben and me, and I want you to keep out of it. You've already done your share, taking Sawbuck off my back this morning. I don't want you mixed up in it any deeper."

"This basin," Kleyburg growled, "is my home range. And any stand I have to take to keep it from being torn to hell and gone, by God, I'll take!"

He opened the corral gate, gave the pinto a slap on the haunch, and sent it through. Howison wiped a sulphur match along the leg of his jeans, cupped the flame in his hands, and bent his head to it. In the small bomb of light, his face showed grave and still. When he pinched out the match, the dark seemed deeper than before.

Henry Kleyburg spoke again, and with an edged vehemence. "The man lied to me, which I can't forgive. He lied to me and played me for a fool, near getting away with it. Just what is Ben Walrode up to, anyhow?"

"Sue asked me that," Howison said. "Here is what I told her."

Kleyburg listened, then burst out strongly again. "If that's it, the man would have to be crazy."

"One word for it," nodded Howison.

"Yet he wanted me to head up his association idea," Kleyburg protested. "Which meant I'd . . ."

"Be the prime target," cut in Howison dryly. "First man down the trail. With a strong chance to be the first to stop lead, should shooting start. A real cozy way to keep covered up personally while getting rid of the most respected and influential man in Jubilee Basin. And to that extent, one of the biggest obstacles against his taking over everything in sight."

He heard Kleyburg's quick inhale of breath, while a shocked awe deepened the cattleman's words.

"Dave — you can't mean that! Walrode wouldn't . . . !"

"Why wouldn't he? When a man's a pirate, a buccaneer at heart, he'll do anything to gain his ends. Once more I say it, Henry. This is my fight, not yours. You keep out of it!"

"It's hard to believe," Kleyburg muttered in that same numbed way. "Hard to believe!" He shook himself and the old, growling truculence returned. "If what you claim is true, then it's a lot more than just your fight."

With Kleyburg so stirred up, Howison knew further argument at this time was useless. He reined his horse around. "Of course I could be borrowing trouble," he temporized. "We'll hope that is so, Henry. Good night!"

Going home, he kept to the same leisurely pace at which he and Sue Kleyburg had covered these same miles earlier. But he rode with thoughts much more grim than then. His final words to Henry Kleyburg were empty, which he knew full well. For all too clearly he recalled the open savagery that had blazed in Ben Walrode as he ordered his men to attack. And all too fiercely had his own bleak fury flamed in return, the embers of it still smoldering. These fires were too primitive, too fundamental and deep-seated ever to be fully extinguished by any amount of wishful thinking.

Ten days ago, even a week ago, nothing so potent had been in the air. Of course his long-time dislike of Ben Walrode was there, yet he had, up until now, managed to cover his feelings fairly well by keeping away from Walrode. But the strong streak of aggressive rapaciousness in Ben Walrode had forced things into the open, and the full measure of the future was any man's guess.

By the time Howison reached home headquarters, Woody Biggs had turned in and the place was dark and still. Howison quietly cared for his horse and as quietly sought his bunk. His bruises were still with him, but the worst of their effects were wearing off, and he found a reasonable ease as he stretched out. The full impact of a rough day's weariness struck quickly and solidly, and he was at the shadowy brink of sleep when the sound reached him across the night's far, dark distance.

So near to slumber, his reactions were sluggish. One part of his muffled mind told him the vagrant sound could have been a gunshot. Another part pushed this thought aside as being of no particular consequence.

Full sleep took over.

CHAPTER

IX

In the ordinary run of daily living, Jock Dunaway was a man of strict habits; the most unvarying of these involved those hours when he sought his blankets at night and when he left them in the morning. Both times were early. In the evening, just as soon as the full shadow of twilight began flowing out from under the Cold River Rim, Dunaway would put supper together for himself and his rider, Joe Ruiz. This eaten, old Jock would sit beside his open doorway long enough to smoke a single pipeful. Then he would turn in.

In part, Joe Ruiz held to the same schedule. He was up at the same early hour as his boss, but being thirty years younger and owning all the vigor of these lesser years, he seldom took to his bunk when Dunaway did. Also, being a full-blooded Shoshone Indian, there were times when the stirring of some deep instinct that had come down to him from his wild heritage would send him riding restlessly under the stars to savor the free spirit of the night.

When he was very young, a malignant fever, striking suddenly and without mercy at an isolated wickiup far out in a Nevada desert, orphaned him. A wandering Basque sheepherder, happening across the place, dug shallow graves for the unfortunate parents and took away with him a half-starved, grief-numbed, six-year-old boy. The sheepherder's first intention had been to leave the forlorn youngster with someone in authority at the next town he came to, but in the interim a deep attachment took hold between the kindly Basque and the black-eyed little Indian lad, and it held them together until the years took their inevitable toll.

The boy was fourteen when his foster father died, leaving him with that father's own name, Joe Ruiz. Now the boy had become a man, and a good one — a rider who knew the cattle trade thoroughly and who had, for several years now, been Jock Dunaway's valued and fully trusted strong right hand.

This night, restless with the old wild stirrings, Indian Joe Ruiz was riding again, drifting quietly through starlight that spread pale silver luster across the world. The breath of the night was good in his nostrils, and way over past the clustered lights of Basin City, Chancellor Peak lifted black and cold against this star glitter.

Sitting easy in the saddle, Indian Joe headed for the upper miles of the basin where a man might more nearly find the isolation his present mood desired. Even so, he could not get completely away from the reminder that other men lived under this same star-strewn sky, for across the chilling distances, lonely gleams of light marked various ranch headquarters.

North and east was Dave Howison's Bar 88 on Bannock Creek. Even farther north stood the Kleyburg ranch, while over north and west, toward Cold River and the black rim rampart beyond, lay Miles Sulivane's tight-fisted layout. Finally, due east, at the base of the foothills below the Sentinels, a light at Price Tedrow's nester cabin made the faintest break against the star-shot dark.

These were things to be noted automatically, as they had been on previous night rides, noted then given no further attention until change came — as it did now, when Sulivane's light winked out, followed later by that at Bar 88, leaving only the

Kleyburg ranch and Tedrow's cabin still holding an identity against the night.

Idle observations, worth but a moment of speculation as now, abruptly, something of more import intruded. Over there to the west, sounded suddenly the soft mutter of hoofs. Alert to every nuance of the night, Joe Ruiz pulled up high and wondering in his saddle, making his judgment. More than one set of hoofs was in yonder travel, moving with a care suggesting secrecy and caution. Wondering who, and why, Joe Ruiz keened the night, eyes and ears straining.

The sound of hoofs slid away, grew fainter, fading toward the west. Interest quickening, Indian Joe followed. The way led to Miles Sulivane's lower holdings along the river flats, and from there down along Jock Dunaway's river range. Also, more than just the mutter of hoofs sounded now. Came the muffled complaint of bedded cattle being roused and put into movement. Joe Ruiz quickened his pace, moving closer.

The complaint of the cattle grew stronger, and dust lifted to put its acrid bite on a man's lips and cheeks. A man's voice, growling, cursed a laggard critter while a rope end slapped hard across a bovine flank. And in the churned up, star-shot dust, cattle and riders were phantom shapes, whirling and shifting.

Ruiz had no gun on him, nor any idea of what the odds could be. But as a man completely faithful to his hire, he did not hesitate. He lifted his horse to a slashing run and charged into the sifting dust. A mounted figure loomed directly ahead.

The impact was heavy, sent both horses floundering, Ruiz's mount going to its knees. But he hauled it up and spurred on at the gather of cattle, lifting a high, shrill yell, hoping to scatter them and start them running.

The rider he had collided with, cursed in dismay and gave shouted warning. "It's Dunaway's man — Indian Joe Ruiz!"

Reply came, swift and wicked, in a voice so gravelly harsh there could be no mistaking its owner.

"Shoot the fool — somebody shoot him!"

Joe Ruiz gave back his defiant answer. "Labine, you can't get away with this!"

Jack Labine's call had come from the left, but it was Nick Bodie who had come in on Ruiz's blind side, stirrup to stirrup, and with drawn gun. From a scant yard of distance Bodie could not miss. Report pounded out, hard and ugly. Tearing through him from side to side, the big .45 slug knocked all the life out of Indian Joe Ruiz in one crashing, deadly moment. He slumped from his saddle, piling up in a huddle against the earth's shocked blackness.

Never a truly brave one, and still shaken from his collision with Ruiz, Chirk Dennis called again, and anxiously.

"That shot could raise hell. Let's get out of here!"

"Not without what we came for," returned Labine harshly. "Get the cattle moving!"

When Tap Geer told Pete Mallory of the final break between Dave Howison and Ben Walrode, he left Pete with plenty to think about, and the more his thoughts played with the subject, the more concerned Pete became. For with the threat of open warfare now spreading an ominous shadow across Jubilee Basin, there was no telling what might come about or who might be hurt.

Just because his own layout was back up here past the Cold River Rim was, as Pete saw it, no guarantee he would be far enough away from any fires of conflict to avoid the full heat of them. Nor did he want to be, not if it meant giving Dave

Howison a helping hand. And sitting back up here, playing it safe, certainly wasn't offering that help.

With this fact in mind, Pete saddled up a little before sundown and headed for Basin City, taking one of the lesser traveled trails that let him down off the rim some miles north of Horsehead Canyon, where he forded the river and rode along into town through the sundown shadows as the clangor of the Cottonwood Hotel supper gong rolled along the street.

Among others, the mellow resonance of the call brought Sheriff Milt Shannon into view; Pete, stepping down and tying at the Ten Strike hitch rail, crossed the street and waited for Shannon on the hotel porch. Shannon eyed him a little warily.

"Now don't you come cryin' to me about anything. I got enough on my mind without any added misery from you."

Pete grinned. "No misery here, Milt — just the milk of human kindness. I was aiming to hold your hand and comfort you."

Shannon grunted sourly. "I don't need anybody to hold my hand or comfort me. Neither do I need anybody to tell me how to run my office. So don't you try. I'm growing a mite weary of people set to run my affairs."

Pete slapped him on the shoulder. "Milt, that's the best thing I've heard from you in I don't know when. Of course that applies to Ben Walrode the same as everybody else?"

"He better believe it does! To Walrode and Howison and Kleyburg and Sulivane — the whole shootin' match. From here on out there's just one sheriff in this basin. That's me!"

"Be darned!" marveled Pete. "Milt, you're gettin' bigger by the minute. I sure admire the looks of you this way. Facts are, I like it so well I'm half a mind to buy you your supper."

The barest flicker of humor loosened the lugubrious set of Milt Shannon's lips. "Make it a whole notion and maybe I can put up with you."

They went in and took a corner table. Shannon slacked down, looked around, then brought his glance back to Mallory.

"For a hard workin' cowman, you're hitting town kind of frequent. Why, Pete?"

Pete told what he had heard from Tap Geer. "Shapes up like the lid might be off. I was wondering what, if anything, was being done to put the fire out. Thought I'd come to town and find out. Maybe you can tell me."

Shannon scrubbed a restless hand across his face. "I aim to do what I can. But those two, Howison and Walrode — I don't see how I can bring them together. Not after that ruckus at Sawbuck. Ain't no place for that affair to go now but downhill. If only Howison had stayed away from out there . . . !"

"From where I stand," said Pete Mallory with emphasis, "Dave Howison is a good man!"

Milt Shannon gave another of his sour grunts. "Suggesting, maybe, that Ben Walrode ain't?"

Pete shrugged. "I go on what I see and hear. That try by Walrode to frame the nester, Price Tedrow, was a pretty crude trick, Milt. Right?"

Shannon nodded wearily. "Made considerable fool of me. I'm still trying to figure why he did it. Don't make good sense."

"Ben Walrode," declared Pete, "is the kind of hombre who does lots of things that don't make good sense to such as you and me, Milt. It's never easy for honest men to follow the tracks of the slickery ones."

Shannon squirmed in his chair. "That's pretty strong talk, cowboy. Maybe I shouldn't be listening to it."

Pete was undaunted. "Show me a hombre who wants to run everybody's business and set himself up as king of the hill, I'll show you one you got to keep a sharp eye on."

"You keep talking," grumbled Shannon, "I won't be able to eat my supper when it gets here. Lay off, will you!"

Pete grinned sardonically. "Milt, you remind me of a bronc that's been loafin' fat and useless in the corral for a long time. And the first time somebody cinches a kak on him and runs a spur rowel up and down his hide, he gets a hump in his back and starts walkin' stiff-legged. But never mind — here comes grub. Eat hearty!"

Supper done with, Shannon produced a couple of cigars, gave Pete one, lit the other himself, and headed back to his office. Pete stood for a little time on the hotel porch, pondering his next move. He had never seen town any quieter than now, so presently, for lack of anything better to do, he headed for Casper's Trading Post on the off chance there might be an item of mail for him.

There wasn't, and after so informing him, Luke Casper eyed the cigar Pete was chewing on and made sarcastic observation.

"Smells like one of Shannon's stogies.

Even so, it's a big improvement over that pipe you usually murder folks with. Man — what a poison pot . . . !"

Pete grinned. "Companion of my best hours, that pipe. You're right about the cigar. Just had supper with Milt and he broke down and turned benevolent."

"Had supper with him, eh? Didn't know you were that fond of him."

Pete sobered. "I'm liking him better. Because he's showing some backbone for a change. He could startle certain folks."

"Which I'll believe when I see it," scoffed Luke skeptically. "Pretty late for a man to straighten up after being hump-backed from packing water on both shoulders for as long as Milt Shannon has."

Pete shrugged. "Maybe so. But I'm giving him benefit of the doubt."

From Casper's, Pete went over to the Ten Strike and found it empty, Cass Garvey puttering at a lot of little nothings behind the bar.

"What's happened to this town?" Pete grumbled. "Never saw it so dead."

"Maybe," said Garvey carefully, "it's scared. When there's trouble in the air, folks tend to hole up in their own teepees."

"What trouble?" demanded Pete. "I don't see any."

"You know what trouble," Garvey said. "You were right in here, backing Dave Howison's hand the other night when him and some of the Sawbuck crew were arguing. There's your trouble."

Pete sighed, hooked both elbows on the bar. "And I hear it's getting worse by the hour. Where's it to end, Cass?"

Considering for a moment, Garvey hunched his shoulders, turned up his hands.

"Smoke rollin', most likely. Comes a day every now and then when there just ain't room enough in all creation for two certain men at the same time. When that happens, one of them has to go. This is that kind of a setup."

"Meaning Dave Howison and Ben Walrode?"

Cass Garvey nodded. "Meanin' them two."

Pete scowled into the back bar mirror. "Sure hate to see it. Particularly where Dave Howison is concerned. I like that man."

"I want no part of it, no matter who's concerned," stated Garvey heavily. "It's like a prairie fire. Starts small, but once it gets to rollin' good it spreads in all directions. Besides bein' bad for business. Speakin' of business, if somebody besides you don't show up pretty quick, I'm closing up to get a real night's sleep for a change. Now did you come in here just to talk, or do you aim to spend a little something?"

Pete made injured protest. "My God, man, I just finished supper. But if you're so money hungry, I'll take you on for a few go-rounds of cribbage. Dollar a game."

Cass Garvey rubbed his hands together. "Cowboy, you got yourself a quarrel!"

They sat at a poker table under the downpouring cone of a hanging lamp's yellow light and marched the pins up and down the board, bickering amiably and slapping the cards hard against the tabletop to emphasize their counting. A stray customer or two drifted in, poured their own drinks, left money on the bar top, and went away. In time, Luke Casper showed for a nightcap and stood watching the play, glass in hand. After he left, it was the roustabout from Treft's stable who came in, poured himself a whiskey, and mumbled a few words over it to everybody in general and no one in particular.

"Thought I heard a gun somewhere up basin a while back. Now, who'd be doin' any shootin' at this time of night?"

Cass Garvey had just died in the hole,

and Pete Mallory, raking in another dollar, was chortling his triumph. So it was that the roustabout's words did not reach far enough to stir any interest. He shrugged, downed his drink, left pay for it, and shuffled out into the night again.

From a center spot on the bottle shelf, a Sessions clock whirred, then beat out eleven measured, bell-toned strokes. Cass Garvey, a three-dollar loser, shoved the cribbage board aside in disgust.

"Darn you, cowboy! You got the devil's own luck. Come by again when your pockets ain't full of horseshoes. Then we'll see."

Pete pushed back his chair, stretching and yawning cheerfully. "Any time, Cass — any time." He jingled his winnings in his palm. "Buy you a drink?"

"Don't want a drink," Garvey growled. "Just sleep. Clear out and let a man get some."

The night breath of Chancellor Peak had come down over town, and Pete Mallory shrugged into the blanket-lined jumper tied to his saddle. His main interest now was to seek the comfort of his own blankets, so he sought the shortest way home, which was by a trail that ran north and west across Jock Dunaway's range. His horse, chilled by hours of inactivity at the Ten Strike hitch rail, stepped out briskly, and Pete, hunching down in the saddle, settled into a half doze.

Several miles later, his horse stopped abruptly, softly snorting, head swinging. Pete straightened in sleepy irritation.

"Blue, you old fool, what's spookin' you?"

Close by, a horse nickered. Pete blinked, then searched the night round about. He tried a short call, but got no answer. A touch of the spur sent Blue reluctantly ahead, only to shift to one side, head outstretched, chuffering nervously. Pete came plenty wide awake now — because Blue was a good horse and a smart one. Something was definitely wrong here.

Again Pete searched the night, and now, in the pale, cold starlight, he made out the other horse. It was riderless.

Chill other than that of the late night rippled up Pete's spine. His probing glance swung here, there. But despite the starlight, the earth's close shadow was too deep for him to be sure of anything from saddle height. So he swung down, holding Blue's rein. He moved cautiously ahead, sending out a short call:

"Hello! Anybody out there?"

No answer came, so he moved carefully on and stumbled over the figure of a man huddled against the earth's blackness.

For a moment, breathless as though struck by a physical blow, Pete froze. Loosening up, for a third time he tested the night for movement or sound. The only move was by the riderless horse, stamping an impatient, worried hoof. The only sound was the far-off yodel of a coyote up along the rim somewhere, which emphasized the abysmal loneliness of a man lying dead against the chilling earth.

Dropping to one knee, Pete lit a match. Its glow against the night was minuscule, but it served the purpose. At what it disclosed, Pete muttered a low, wondering curse that carried the beginnings of a harsh outrage. He climbed back in his saddle, reined Blue around, and headed once more for town. The riderless horse nickered after him anxiously, but Pete figured it would still be there, faithful to the tie of grounded reins, when he returned.

Town, when he entered it this time, was completely dark and silent. He hauled up at the Cottonwood Hotel, then took off his spurs before tiptoeing through the lobby and up the stairs to Milt Shannon's room. The sheriff was sawing wood blissfully, but roused quickly when Pete shook him and warned him softly.

"Easy does it, Milt. This is Mallory. On the way home I found a dead man by the trail. That Indian puncher of Jock Dunaway's. He'd been shot. Figured you'd want to know and maybe need some help in bringing him in."

The words hit like a dash of cold water. Shannon threw aside his blankets. "Get a light going, so I can see what I'm doing."

Pete lit the lamp on the table beside the bed, and while Milt Shannon dressed, went over his report in a little more detail. Shannon listened wordlessly, then bent to pull on his boots.

"Go down to Treft's livery and kick that roustabout awake. He sleeps in the harness room. Tell him I'll want a team and spring wagon. Better throw in a couple of blankets, too. I'll be right along."

The wagon was waiting when the sheriff arrived. Pete left Blue to be grained and curried, and took up the reins of the team. With Milt Shannon settled in morose silence beside him, he swung the team out of town at a trot. After a time, he spoke his somber thoughts.

"How do you figure it, Milt?"

"I don't," came the sour answer. "Because

that Indian was a good man. Never caused anybody a lick of trouble. So who would want to shoot him? Some more darn business that don't make sense."

At the scene of death, all was as Pete had left it. The body of Indian Joe Ruiz was still a dark bundle against the earth, and his faithful horse still waited, loose reins dragging.

It was rough business, getting the dead man into the wagon. When it was done, Pete went to get the waiting horse. He stood for a little time, petting it, while it nuzzled him in relief. He tied it at lead behind the wagon, climbed in and took up the reins once more. And when he entered Basin City yet again, thoroughly weary and depressed, he realized that the night had run out and that up past Chancellor Peak and the Sentinels, a new dawn was beginning to filter across the world.

As they pulled into the stable runway, Pete said: "I promised Tap Geer that if anything like this broke, I'd get the word to Dave Howison right away. You got any objections, Milt?"

Shannon grunted. "No! Why should I? Can't keep a thing of this sort secret, and no good reason for trying to. The more people hear about it and get stirred up, the quicker, maybe, we find the answer."

CHAPTER

X

In the first flush of morning, Tap Geer began to stir. His couch for the night had been the hard, hard earth, his cover a single blanket that had not entirely warded off the deepened chill of the early hours. His first drowsy thought was that these combined discomforts were what had brought him awake. Then he realized that it was something more. It was noise.

The lingering dregs of sleep, plus a puzzled wondering, held Tap in his blanket for a little time. Then he rolled clear, pulled on his boots, and got to his feet, shrugging off night's stiffness. At the end of its picket rope yonder, his horse stood with ear-pricked, inquiring head. And in the lava wilderness, out somewhere past the limits of this little clearing, lifted the steady complaint of tired cattle.

What cattle? Whose cattle? Why were they out there now when there had been neither sign nor sound of them yesterday

190

afternoon or last night? True, he had jumped a pair of wild ones from this clearing, but there had to be a lot more than two out under that sound.

Yeah, what cattle? Whose cattle?

Well, he had come into this pothole country looking for possible answers to certain things, and here might be one . . .

He brought in and saddled his horse, then rolled and packed his meager outfit. And then, on foot, rifle in hand, he went to investigate.

The country hadn't changed a bit; it was just like yesterday: jagged lava ridges to skirt or climb over, with endless thickets of tangled mahogany brush to fight a way through. In this country, a man watched his step or he could easy end up with a broken leg . . .

Sound of the cattle increased. A lava ridge, higher than most, lifted to bar his way. The face of it was steep, its fangs jagged and cruel. Tap climbed it carefully and from its crest, where a fringe of mahogany brush sheltered him, had his look.

Ahead was a good-sized flat that in winter would hold a shallow sheet of water, but which now was a dry lake bed. Cattle milled about on it, stirring up a haze of alkali dust. Some fifty or sixty head, Tap judged. Holding the cattle were several riders, and Tap wished for morning's light to quicken so that he might perhaps identify some of these.

His chance came presently when a wilder one of the herd made a break and a rider spurred to turn it back. The maneuver swung both animal and rider by within fifty scant yards of Tap's hiding place. What he saw left him still and breathless. Even in this gray morning light a man would have had to been blind to mistake or misread the bold slash of the brand that the steer carried. It was Claymore, Jock Dunaway's iron. But the rider was Chirk Dennis of Sawbuck!

A Claymore critter, a Sawbuck rider!

Tap's thoughts raced. They raced even faster as the steadily brightening sky lifted more and more of the world out of shadow. Now he could identify others of the riders. Two of them were Jack Labine and Nick Bodie. But even this did not startle him as did sure recognition of still another of the group. There was no mistaking that lean, swarthy-faced figure, a man with whom he had once shared his fire and his coffee.

Jett Chesbro! And right now talking with Jack Labine and apparently on the best of terms with him . . .

Tap stared and stared again. Here indeed was one of the answers he had come to the pothole country to find. And one to get to the ears of Dave Howison as quickly as possible. He took a final look to make sure he wasn't dreaming, then dropped back down off the ridge and headed back to his camp, breaking into a run when he reached the clearing where his horse waited. Quickly in the saddle, he headed north, backtracking along the same way he had entered the potholes.

What he had just witnessed, along with the enormity of its possible significance, built up such an edge of hurry it took a scrambling stumble by his willing, hard-working horse to jar some sense of caution into him, and he let his mount slack to a saner pace. After all, an hour or two in time now wouldn't make much difference. This word he was carrying was so big, its limits so ominous, it could never be lost in time. For sure, Jubilee Basin was in for a showdown such as it had never known before.

The sun came up and spread its warmth, and along with his horse, Tap began to sweat — the horse from pure physical effort, he from the press of a driving impatience. But you couldn't compress time, and you couldn't compress distance. It became just a question of riding out the miles.

Which he did, and finally there was Horsehead Canyon opening before him. He slanted down its south side, let his mount snatch a short drink at the river, then pushed on across and up the far side to the road. Here he met the stage on its outgoing run. As the old Concord clacked by, rocking and creaking on its leather thorough braces, Buck Pruitt gave him a wondering stare and saluted him halfheartedly with a raised whip.

Tap ignored the move and sent his sarcastic mutter after the speeding vehicle.

"Take a real good look, you ory-eyed old gossip! And I'm plenty south of Big Stony, which you can tell Ben Walrode and be damned to both of you! Because I'm packing news like you never heard before . . . !"

Daybreak at Bar 88 found Dave Howison enormously stiff and sore, yet mobile. He grimaced as he took careful seat across the breakfast table from Woody Biggs, but found that whatever his physical discomfort, there was nothing wrong with his appetite, a fact that moved Woody to pointed remark.

"Man who can eat like you ain't got too

much wrong with him."

Howison grinned. "I keep telling you I'm well past the coddling age."

"Mebbe so," allowed Woody. "But you sure ain't reached the age of real good sense, yet. You had, you wouldn't have to grunt and groan when you sit up to your victuals."

About to reply, Howison cocked a listening head. "Rider coming in."

Woody got up and went to the door, presently calling greeting. "Hiyah, Pete! Riding a little far and early, ain't you? Light down, breakfast's on the table." Then as Pete Mallory came in, he added: "You look kinda gaunt and empty, like you mighta seen a hard night."

"Too hard," returned Pete gruffly. "If I look bad, it's because that's the way I feel."

"Must be a reason," Howison said, eyeing him keenly.

"A good one," said Pete, dropping into a chair. "I just come out from town, after helpin' Milt Shannon haul a dead man in off the range."

Howison's concern was quick. "Devil you say! Who?"

"That Indian rider of Dunaway's — Joe Ruiz. Somebody shot him. Figured you'd like to know."

All humor and ease left Howison. He leaned forward, his words clipped. "Let's have it."

Woody put some breakfast before Mallory and Pete, while he ate, told his somber story.

"Sure startled me," he ended. "Stumblin' across a dead man in the dark that way."

Woody Biggs said the same thing Milt Shannon had. "Who'd want to shoot Indian Joe? He was a good one, never no bother to anybody."

Howison's thoughts were bleak and had him scowling. "No sign of anything else around, Pete — just Joe's body, and his horse?"

"All I saw," nodded Pete. "Of course it was deep night, and dark."

"Well, it's light now," Howison said. "You and me, we're riding back out there."

"Think I'll go along," said Woody.

"No!" Howison said it evenly, but there was authority behind it. "Your place is here, Woody. Pete and I can handle this."

In ways that did not count overly much, Woody could often win his point with his boss. But this was not one of them, and he knew it. However, he added one stroke of warning. "This kind of business is Milt

Shannon's responsibility. Don't you go gettin' proud and take it on yourself to do his job for him."

Howison dropped a placating hand on the old fellow's shoulder. "I won't. I know my limits."

"Me," said Pete, "I could use a fresh bronc. Mine's been traveling all over, all night long, seems like."

They caught up a fresh mount for Pete, and Howison saddled his big buckskin. He slung a Winchester under his stirrup leather and buckled on a belt gun, preparations that Woody Biggs eyed with mixed feelings.

"Darn, boy," he grumbled, "I sure hate to see you dressin' up this way. Still and all, the way things are going, you could be plumb naked without a gun."

They started off through morning's first cool, clear light, but as they moved out across the basin's wide floor, the sun peered over the crest of the Sentinels to throw their shadows ahead of them, slanting and jagged. So far as Howison could see, they had the main run of the basin to themselves. Sometime later a thought came to him, and he voiced it.

"Wonder has Jock Dunaway been notified?"

"Not unless Milt Shannon sent some-body out," Pete said.

Leading the way, Pete struck the trail he had traveled last night and headed along it, glance alert and searching as they cut down the miles. They were only a little way short of Cold River when he finally reined up and pointed.

"Right there, Dave."

A dark smear marked the place where the blood of Indian Joe Ruiz had stained the dusty earth. Green flies were swarming over it. Howison's glance touched the spot briefly, then swung to take in a larger area. All round about the earth was trampled and cut. He circled back and forth a few times before pulling in beside Mallory again.

"What do you think, Pete?"

"Looks to me like somebody had bunched a fair-sized jag of cattle here, then moved them down river," Pete decided.

Howison nodded. "Just so. And it's a fair guess that Indian Joe caught up with who-ever was doing it, and they shot him. Now that I think of it, I heard that shot last night. I'd turned in and was almost asleep. It sounded faint and far out, the shot did, but I heard it."

He looked around again, his glance

narrowed and brooding as though setting up a mind picture of last night's grim happening. Abruptly he asked:

"When you found him, Pete, did Indian Joe have a gun on him?"

"No sign of one. No belt, not even a saddle gun."

"Then they shot an unarmed man. Which could mean several things."

"Like such?" asked Pete.

Howison shook his head. "Have to think on that. Let's get along to town."

"Mebbe we should go see what Jock Dunaway has to say," Pete suggested.

Howison shook his head again. "Jock's too old a man to mix in running down this thing. That's Milt Shannon's chore. And I want to know what he intends to do about it."

The word was out in town, and Basin City was stirring uneasily. Milt Shannon was in his office, talking with Doc Church, and looking a little more seedy and tired than usual. At sight of Howison, and recognizing the temper in him, Shannon spoke quickly and defensively.

"I'm just as mad as you are, Dave. I liked Indian Joe. I don't know who killed him, or why, but I sure aim to have one hell of a try at finding out. Now that it's daylight, I'm riding out to where it happened and see if I can pick up some sort of sign to start on."

"You don't need to," Howison told him. "Pete and I just came from there, and we got your lead for you. It figures somebody was helping themselves to a gather of cattle, and Joe Ruiz caught them at it." He turned to Doc Church. "You've examined Joe, Doc?"

Doc nodded. "I'm taking care of him."

"Anything strike you as unusual? I mean in physical effect."

Doc Church pursed his lips, shook his head slowly. "No-o. I doubt the poor devil knew what hit him."

"Six-gun or rifle?"

"The first. Heavy caliber. Forty-four or forty-five."

Howison considered a moment, eyes pinched. "From how far away would you say?"

"Quite close. His shirt was powder burnt. The bullet went completely through."

"Then," said Howison quickly, "he could have been close enough to recognize who shot him, even in the dark?"

"That is so," affirmed Doc.

"Doc and I were talking about that very

angle when you came in," Shannon said. "It's something to think about, all right."

"More than just think about," returned Howison bleakly. "Milt, I'm riding with you. Let's go see where the trail of that gather of cattle leads to!"

"Me," said Pete Mallory, "I'm beginnin' to run a little short on sleep, but I'll shag along."

Milt Shannon shook his head. "No need, Pete. But you can go out to Claymore and tell Jock Dunaway what happened. Make it as easy as you can on the old fellow."

Pete was still reluctant. "No tellin' what you and Dave could run into, and need a little help."

Shannon scowled irritably as he stood up. "Told you last evening I didn't need anybody to hold my hand. Maybe I been some slack in the past, and not too smart in some ways. But there's more to Milt Shannon than you think. You do as I say; go give Jock Dunaway the word. Dave and me, we'll trail the cattle and take care of whatever it leads us to."

There was a tall cupboard against one wall of the room. From a shelf of this, Milt Shannon lifted down a holstered gun, wrapped in a cartridge belt. He unwound the belt, buckled it on, settled it firmly about his hips, then snapped out the gun with a speed that made Pete Mallory blink. Observing, Shannon smiled thinly.

"I cut my eye teeth at this star-packing trade a long time ago, Pete. I've handled my share of tough ones, and can do it again. People sometimes get funny ideas about men like me. Just because we don't spit nails or wear barbwire britches they figure we don't rate much. And they been wrong a lot of times." He holstered the gun, then slapped the butt of it. "One of these, when you know how to handle it, and backed by the star, sure strikes up a strong average. All right, Dave. If we're riding, let's be about it."

They saddled a mount at the livery for Shannon, then cut due west to pick up the trail of the driven cattle. It was plainly marked, following the run of the river flats for a considerable distance before swinging east to cross Big Stony Creek just above the bridge and driving straight on south toward the far pothole country.

Shannon stared at the distant lava badlands. "Heading for Jett Chesbro country, Dave. Maybe Ben Walrode was right in warning of something like this when he talked organization. Maybe we should have listened to him."

"You're jumping at conclusions again, Milt," Howison told him. "From all I've heard, Jett Chesbro does have a liking for other men's cattle. But I've never heard him rated as a killer. And right now we're out to run down somebody who is a killer as well as a thief."

Shannon frowned over this for a moment or two, then grunted morosely. "Damn such a business!"

They went steadily on, and as they drew even with Horsehead Canyon, a rider emerged from the mouth of it, traveling the road to town. It was Tap Geer and he was pushing right along. He was too far away to hail vocally, but when Howison stood high in his stirrups and waved his hat, Tap caught the move, stared for a moment, then came toward them, his horse at a run. Both horse and rider were sweating and showed signs of wear and tear as they came pounding up.

"Man, oh man!" exulted Tap. "Am I glad to see you two! Saves time, and right now time can be plenty valuable."

Howison eyed him searchingly. "Thought I told you to stay away from this deadline country and the chance of trouble. What are you doing down here, and what are you so excited about?"

"About something I had to look at two or three times just to be certain I wasn't seeing things," retorted Tap. "Milt, what would you say if I told you the Sawbuck outfit were a flock of cow thieves?"

Shannon stared. "What would I say? Why, either you're drunk or loco. What the devil you driving at?"

"I just told you. That Sawbuck gang are cow thieves. And I can prove it."

Now Shannon measured Tap with more care. "All right," he growled curtly. "I'm listening."

"Here's what I saw early this morning on a dry lake out in the pothole country," Tap began. As he went along with his story, he glimpsed the shadow of doubt in Shannon and burst out half angrily, "Milt — don't look at me like that! I didn't dream this up. I tell you I saw it plain as plain — no mistake, no guessing. At least one critter in that herd wore Jock Dunaway's Claymore iron, and all three Sawbuck hands were there. Labine, Dennis, and Bodie. Labine, he was talking real friendly with Jett Chesbro, like they were closing out a deal of some sort." Tap turned to Howison. "Do you believe me, Dave?"

"All the way, boy," Howison said. "Yeah, all the way. Because it ties in. Because it fits the killing angle exactly."

"Killing!" blurted Tap. "What killing?"

Howison explained tersely. "So, by all the signs, Indian Joe Ruiz caught them at their little game, recognized them, and they shot him."

Tap flared bitterly. "Dirty whelps! Indian Joe was a better man than all that crowd put together. Milt, you'll be going after them — after that Sawbuck crowd?"

"Not quite so fast," Shannon said. "You say Labine, Bodie, and Dennis were there. But you didn't see Ben Walrode?"

Tap shook his head. "If he was there, he wasn't bunched with the others. There were three or four strangers, guys I'd never seen before. They were scattered around, holding the cattle. Probably Chesbro's men. But just because Walrode wasn't around, doesn't mean he wasn't in on it somewhere. He was behind trying to frame Price Tedrow on that slow-elking deal, and he's behind this rustling deal."

Milt Shannon considered it all in head-bent silence. Then he scrubbed a weary hand across his face, speaking slowly. "All this, I hate to believe. But it looks like I got to. Dave, we'll head for Sawbuck now. Because while rustling is bad, murder is a lot worse. The cattle and Jett Chesbro can wait for another day."

"If Chesbro wants to really drive 'em, you'll never see any of those cattle again," declared Tap. "Or see Chesbro, either, for that matter. Because that pothole country is really big and wild. I can be happy to stay out of it from now on. But long as you're heading for Sawbuck, I'll go along. I want to see the look on Ben Walrode's face when you brace him. Him and his deadline! No wonder he didn't want me prowling this stretch of range. He was scared I'd see exactly what I did see. And all the time him acting so high and righteous about organizing against rustlers! Dave, it's like you said about that medicine man in Winnemucca. Get people watching your left hand while you do the big monkey business with your right. Well, that's Ben Walrode for you, Milt. Let's go get him!"

"Not you, boy," said Shannon. "I don't want to risk a star witness getting hurt, should things turn dirty at Sawbuck. You know what you saw, and now Dave and I know, too. But should anything happen to you, I wouldn't have a real court case against anybody. Nothing I could prove. Because all I'd have is hearsay, which ain't worth a darn as evidence. But with you there to testify in person, I can cinch any of that crowd I bring in.

"So you head on into town and stay there. And keep your mouth shut. Understand? Don't tell anybody what you just told us. Should they ask where you been and doing what, tell 'em anything you want — except the truth. No argument, now! I'm running this show, and you do as I say."

Tap looked at the sheriff in some surprise. Here was a Milt Shannon who sat considerably taller in the saddle than he had the last time Tap saw him.

"All right," Tap sighed. "All right, Milt. I'll do like you say. But you two watch it — watch it careful! Remember that someone in that crowd killed Indian Joe. Which means they'll kill again if they have to."

"We'll watch it," Shannon said grimly. "That I can promise you. Now scatter along and behave yourself."

CHAPTER

XI

It was past mid-morning when Jack Labine, Nick Bodie, and Chirk Dennis, holding close beneath the southern reach of the Sentinels and riding hard, got back to Sawbuck headquarters. Leaving Bodie and Dennis to care for the weary, ridden-out horses, Labine, with saddlebag in hand, headed for the ranch office where Ben Walrode waited.

There was a growling eagerness in Walrode's greeting. "How did things go?"

"So-so." Labine tossed the saddlebag on Walrode's desk. "Little better than two thousand in there. We turned sixty-eight head over to Chesbro, and he paid thirty a head, straight across."

Walrode pulled the saddlebag to him and began opening it. "I thought we might do better than sixty-eight head. What was wrong — weren't the cattle bunched along the river flats like we figured they would be?"

"The cattle were there all right," Labine

told him. "But so was Dunaway's rider, Indian Joe Ruiz. How he happened to show, I don't know. But there he was. After he was taken care of, we had to move fast with just what stock we'd already picked up."

Walrode exclaimed, "Ruiz — taken care of! You mean you . . . ?"

Labine shrugged. "We couldn't let him go spread the word, could we? There was only one way to handle it. Nick gunned him."

"That," said Walrode heavily, "was a bad break. Somebody will find him. And then . . ."

"Sure they'll find him," Labine cut in. "They'll also find sixty-eight head of cattle missing. But the trail of the cattle leads straight into the pothole badlands. Which points everything at Jett Chesbro, which Jett understands. He's not worried, so why should we be?"

Walrode's worried scowl lightened a little. "If you're sure nobody else saw you . . . ?"

"Nobody did," Labine assured. "Except for Ruiz, everything went smooth, with no sign of alarm anywhere. We're in the clear, Ben. We delivered the stock and we got our money. Jett, he's got a layout that will take over the cattle way down in the Dixie

Valley country. He'll be gone a couple or three months, then be back to talk business again. All we got to do is sit tight, stay close to home, and wait for things to quiet down once more. After they do, we can figure on another good chunk of the same kind of business."

"Sounds all right," Walrode conceded. "Just the same, it pays to be sure. I think we should have somebody drift into town and listen in on any talk going around."

"Suits me," Labine nodded. "I'll send Bodie. Nobody will run Nick out like they did Dennis. If that smart pup, Geer, wants to try his luck with Nick, let him."

"Not that, either," Walrode ordered. "We're strictly on our own now, and the quieter we stay and the less fuss we stir up, the better. Send Bodie in, but tell him to go easy."

From a desk drawer, Walrode produced bottle and glasses. He poured the drinks and pushed one over to Labine. "To more easy beef, Jack!"

A streak of dark, sardonic humor in Jack Labine erupted into harsh laughter. "More easy beef — and a couple of scalps along the way!"

"Right! In particular — Howison's!" As he said it, Walrode's mouth shaped to its most sullen, ugly cast.

"Keno!" seconded Labine. "That, we'll drink to."

On first thought, Nick Bodie viewed the prospect of a ride to town with anything but pleasure, as he had just come in from a sleepless night in the saddle. Yet there was an angle that beckoned. Whiskey! In town, at the Ten Strike, there would be plenty of it. So, without too much reluctance, he caught up a fresh mount and rode out, taking the shorter saddle trail along the base of Chancellor Peak and across the upper reaches of Big Stony Creek, a route that put him out of sight from Dave Howison and Milt Shannon — and they from him — as they crossed the lower end of the basin from the main road and moved in on Sawbuck headquarters.

"I've a feeling about this, Dave, so watch it!" warned Shannon. "Let me do the talking."

Howison had a feeling of his own. It was a current across his nerve ends, honing every instinct in him to a taut, vibrant edge. It sharpened all outlines and made all sounds distinct, building an alertness in him that put him high and wary in his saddle.

They were in the area between the ranch

house and the rest of the layout when Ben Walrode stepped into view. He scowled as he came toward them, throwing out his heavy arrogance.

"What's the idea, Shannon, bringing Howison in here? You should know he's not welcome on my land."

"Hadn't thought of it quite that way," returned Shannon mildly, his glance touching here and there. "Where are your riders, Ben?"

"Somewhere around. What about them?"

"Want to see them. Call them out."

"Want to see them about what?"

"Few questions to ask."

"While I want Howison off my land," laid out Walrode roughly. "With me, that comes first."

"Not today." Shannon's tone turned crisp. He stepped down from his saddle. "Quit stalling, Ben. Get your men out here, or I root them out!"

Jack Labine sauntered from the bunkhouse. "Won't be necessary, Milt."

"The others?" demanded Shannon. "Bodie and Dennis — where are they?"

"Why Nick, he's gone to town to get the mail. And Chirk, he's inside, sewin' a button on his shirt."

There was a mockery in Labine's words

that he did not try to hide, but Shannon ignored it. Because over in a corral were three gaunt and plainly hard-ridden broncs on whom the saddle sweat had hardly dried. Shannon indicated these with a tip of his head.

"Ben, those broncs yonder must have been covering a considerable amount of trail. Your men always do so much riding this early in the day?"

There was the faintest shade of hesitancy in Walrode, so it was Jack Labine who answered. "Here at Sawbuck we like to get most of our saddle work done before it gets too hot."

"Well then, Jack, where did you ride to this morning?" probed Shannon.

Labine shrugged nonchalantly. "Where does a puncher usually ride when he's about ranch chores? Here, there — round about."

"Never saw broncs sweated out that bad, doing just a few morning chores," observed Shannon. "Those yonder look to me like they might have been traveling all night. Are you sure they weren't, Jack?"

Labine swung back a step or two, and in his eyes, far back, little crimson fires began to spark. When he spoke, his gravel-toned words fell cold and bitter.

"Milt, you're driving at something. What is it?"

"I think you know, Jack," Shannon told him, almost softly. "You, too, Ben. And you're both under arrest!"

Jack Labine's breath came out of him in a thin hiss as he rolled upon his toes. With quick, blurted speech, Walrode headed him off.

"You gone crazy, Shannon? Why would you want to arrest us? What for?"

"Long as you ask, Ben, one count is cattle stealing. The other is for the murder of Indian Joe Ruiz!" Shannon gave it to him bluntly. "I'm taking you in."

It couldn't last, after that. Dave Howison knew it, Milt Shannon knew it. For while Ben Walrode might have tried further talk, with Jack Labine all time for talk had run out. The basic makeup of this man was too primitive, too wild and contentious to ever temporize long. He might ride a bluff for a time, but only so far, and this one, he now knew, was no good. Somehow, somewhere, Milt Shannon had learned the truth of last night.

As Jack Labine saw life, a man lived or died by his acceptance of facts when these were beyond denial. This quick acceptance, and an equally quick reaction had, on several grim occasions at other times and other places along a somewhat murky trail of living, won him clear. Knowing no other solution, he now reached for the only one he did know. He reached for his gun.

He got there fast — very fast. Too fast for Milt Shannon, too fast for Dave Howison. Too fast in fact for the sure kill he had intended, and the bullet — a little high, a little wide — plowed through Shannon's shoulder instead of his heart. But the impact knocked the sheriff flat and Labine, seeing him go down, had his next try at Dave Howison.

The blare of Labine's first shot startled Howison's horse; the big buckskin was rearing as Labine shot again, and the slug that might otherwise have drilled into Dave Howison's vitals, smashed instead into the swell fork of his saddle. It tore through tough, bullhide leather and buried against the hickory saddle tree beneath, and though untouched, Howison felt the shock all through him.

At Labine's first hostile move, Howison had gone for his own gun, and the split second of grace now allowed him because of Labine's miss enabled him to make his try. Even as the gun bucked in recoil, the horse under him was whirling, a move that put his back to Labine. Desperately he hauled the animal on around, his stomach a cold knot in expectation of another shot from Labine.

But Jack Labine wasn't doing any more shooting. Instead, he was down on one knee, head bent, almost like a man at prayer, his gun fallen from a hand gone limp. Now, even as Howison watched, Jack Labine toppled over on his face, one lank leg extended, the other doubled under him. A booted foot drummed the earth twice, then was still.

Reaction held Howison frozen. This sort of thing never had been any real part in his life. On occasion he had speculated what he might do, how he might react, what his feelings would be should such necessity ever strike. Now it had happened and all of it had been so fast, so starkly savage and desperate, he had had no time to wonder or speculate. He had only time to act.

And it was done. He had just killed a man, and his only feeling was a sort of numbed inability to accept the stark reality of it. For this bleak moment he made a still, open target, and Ben Walrode, features convulsed in a mixture of hate, fear, and dark purpose, brought a shoulder gun from under his jumper and pulled down for a dead sure shot.

Down but not out, Milt Shannon hauled his gun with his sound hand and shot Ben Walrode through the head, even as he called warning. "The other two, Dave — watch for them! The other two . . . !"

Shannon's shot and now his warning cry brought Howison out of his saddle, gun poised and ready. Over at the door of the bunkhouse there was furtive movement, and Howison dropped his weapon in line with it. But when Chirk Dennis stepped out, he had both hands half raised and empty, and he called with fear-thickened words:

"Hold it — hold it! I'm not in this thing — not in it — !"

"Bodie!" Howison rapped. "Where's Nick Bodie — ?"

"Town," blurted Dennis. "Like Labine said — in town."

He stumbled uncertainly, as though his heavy legs had become uncoordinated, and he stared at the crumpled figures of Ben Walrode and Jack Labine with slack-jawed, bleared fascination.

"Knew it would be like this," he mumbled. "I told them the shootin' of that rider of Dunaway's would bring on trouble. That Nick Bodie, he did it. He shot Indian Joe Ruiz. I — I helped with the cattle, but I never shot nobody — I never did!"

Milt Shannon, recovering somewhat, called harshly, "Don't trust him, Dave! He makes one bad move, nail him!"

If Dennis had a gun on him anywhere, Howison could not see it. He motioned with his own weapon. "Over there!" he ordered. "And stay put. You make that bad move, it will be like Shannon says."

Dennis sagged on his heels, still mumbling. "I tell you I'm quittin'. I want no more of this."

Howison moved over to Milt Shannon, who was propped up on his right elbow. His left arm hung limp against him, and the shoulder of his coat had become dark and soggy. The sheriff's face was pale, his lips pulled thin.

"Maybe you better tie me up a little, Dave — before I leak completely dry. That Labine — he was fast as a snake. I thought I could beat him, but he was way ahead of me — way ahead!"

Howison got Shannon's coat off and with his pocket knife cut away the shirt beneath. He wadded pieces of the shirt against the wound and tied them there with his neckerchief. He hung Shannon's coat back over the crippled shoulder.

"You're for town and Doc Church,

Milt," he said gruffly. "Just hang on for a little while."

He flung a hard order at Chirk Dennis. "Hook a team to the spring wagon. I'll be watching — close! You keep a whole skin only if you do exactly as you're told. Now move! Make it fast."

Chirk Dennis made it fast. He was completely subdued. The crashing end to Ben Walrode and Jack Labine had left him empty of everything but fear. With Howison watching, he brought the spring wagon over beside Shannon and gave a hand in getting the wounded lawman into the rig.

"You drive," Howison told him bleakly. "You drive fast, but careful. You make it as easy on Shannon as you can. I'll be riding right behind you. You may get a break in this if you do as you're told."

Chirk Dennis had a final look at Walrode and Labine.

"What about them?" he asked dully. "Them two — you leavin' them — just leavin' them?"

"For now, yes," Howison told him coldly. "Indian Joe was just left, wasn't he? Get the rig moving!"

CHAPTER

XII

From a favorite vantage point, which was a
chair in front of Luke Casper's Trading Post,
Tap Geer watched Basin City writhe and
squirm as it absorbed the ominous import of
a rustling raid and the shooting down of an
unarmed, well-liked cowhand. The word
had spread fast. Pete Mallory had carried it
to Jock Dunaway and Miles Sulivane, and
from there it had reached Henry Kleyburg.
Now these cattlemen and numerous citizens
of the town were gathered in the Ten Strike,
Kleyburg and Sulivane fuming and militant.

Jock Dunaway, a kindly man who had
lost a good friend and faithful hand in
Indian Joe Ruiz, was more stunned than
anything else. Loss of cattle hurt, of
course, but these could be replaced by time
and the processes of nature. But Indian Joe
could not be brought back, and this fact
bowed the old cattleman's shoulders and
shrouded his mind in a gray, weary grief.
Just a little bit ago, Tap had watched the

old Scotchman cross the street with slow steps and felt a rush of sympathy for him and a renewed gust of outrage toward Ben Walrode, his outfit, and all its crooked workings.

On his return to town after meeting Dave Howison and Milt Shannon at the mouth of Horsehead Canyon, Tap had slipped into Basin City quietly and taken post there in front of Luke Casper's place of business until Howison and Shannon should return. Until then, true to his promise to Shannon, Tap vowed to keep his momentous news to himself — though he couldn't help speculating what the result would be should he walk into the Ten Strike right now and lay the true word in front of Henry Kleyburg and Miles Sulivane and the rest. He, Tap Geer, made a virtual pariah by Ben Walrode's lies, was now able to throw the lies right back into the teeth of men who had chosen to believe them.

Earlier, Luke Casper had come out to discuss the news, then had gone back inside to take care of a customer. Now he came out again to stand beside Tap, speaking slowly.

"You, Mister Geer, are sure one slickery son-of-a-gun. But you don't fool me, playing it so close-mouthed the way you're doing. You got a cat-and-canary look about you that you just can't hide from old Luke. You're just plain bustin' with something you know, but aim to keep to yourself, for some fool reason. You sneaked out of town real quiet, and you sneaked back in, real quiet. And when a friend — that's me — Luke Casper, asks where you been and doin' what, you come up with hocus-pocus talk of being off trying to knock over a deer.

"Hell! You and Barney Tuttle ain't ate up the last one you got. And you're not that full of ambition you'd go lookin' for another until you turn real hungry again. So, right now you better start tellin' me the truth before I throw you out in the street."

"You," retorted Tap, "are the most suspicious, gossipy, prying old biddy I know. Man can't turn around without you getting all worked up and curious. Just plain scared to death you might miss something, that's you. You ought to be wearing a dress instead of that apron."

"Still skittering around, ducking and dodging, that's you," returned Luke calmly. "Still lyin' like a trooper. But I'll get the truth out of you if it takes me all day!"

Up street, Allie Langley stepped from the Cottonwood Hotel and came along, big market basket on her arm. As she climbed the steps to the store, Tap stood up and touched his hat.

"Fine day, Mrs. Langley!"

She paused, eyeing him with mock disapproval. "Tap Geer, if you don't quit hanging around so much, you'll turn into a confirmed loafer. You ought to be ashamed."

"Exactly what I been telling him, Allie," put in Luke quickly. "All he ever does is just aggravate people."

Allie Langley smiled gently. A widowed woman who had made her own way in the world for many years, she had amassed a considerable store of wisdom and tolerance in balancing people's virtues against their faults, thereby arriving at a fairly satisfactory total.

"Oh, I don't think Tap is such a total loss, Luke."

Tap grinned. "Know something, Mrs. Langley? I been taking a good look at myself, and I think you're right. I aim to line me up a steady job and turn plumb respectable."

"Hah!" grunted Luke. "Cold day that'll be!" Saying which, he followed Mrs. Langley inside.

As Tap resumed his seat, the sound of hoofs in the street drew his glance. What he saw almost brought him to his feet again. The rider was Nick Bodie, coming along at a driving jog. For a breath or two, Tap went a little panicky, his thoughts whirling. Because this didn't add up. With Dave Howison and Milt Shannon gone out to Sawbuck for the avowed purpose of taking Ben Walrode and his crew into custody, here was one of the roughest of the Sawbuck hands riding into town in apparent unconcern.

What had gone wrong? How had Howison and Shannon missed this fellow Bodie? What, if anything, had happened out at Sawbuck? Or could something have happened that was dark and ominous?

These, and a dozen other half-formed surmises and guesses spun through Tap's mind as Nick Bodie pulled in at the Ten Strike hitch rail, got down, and tied. But Bodie did not go into the saloon. Instead, he came angling over to the Trading Post. He was a burly one, Nick Bodie, guttural of speech and full of a hot, easily aroused animalism. He paused in front of Tap.

"Want to try your hand at running me out of town, Geer?"

All manner of retort hovered on Tap's

tongue, but he did a good job of holding back the more reckless ones.

"I'm busy, right now, minding my own business," he returned.

"Smart boy," taunted Bodie. "Real smart boy!"

He went on into the Trading Post.

Tap's thoughts brought a surge of bile spilling up into his throat. Cow thief! Big with your talk now, Bodie, but if you knew what I know — what I know!

Tap shook himself. Sure, Geer, you know plenty! But right now just thinking about it — and talking to yourself — isn't enough. Not near enough! Come alive and do something about this. Really do something . . . !

The same fire that had flamed when he took care of Chirk Dennis began to burn again in Tap. Bodie was a tough one, all right, and no doubt a bad one with a gun. Tap, though he knew he could hold his own any time, any place with a Winchester, also knew he was no hand with a belt gun. Never had been, never wanted to be. So he would be a plain fool to try going with one against such as Bodie. And, good as he was with a rifle, in a close up deal it was a lot slower handling than a six-gun.

Yet he had to do something. He couldn't allow Bodie to ride into town and out again like an honest man on honest business. This fellow was outlaw — bad outlaw. And likely enough, bad killer besides. So he had to be stopped. But how . . . ?

Then it came to Tap, and he was up with the thought and moving in a soft-footed hurry. He dropped off the far end of the Trading Post platform, ducked past the corner of the place, and lit out at a run, threading the back areas of town over to Barney Tuttle's cabin.

In older, still wilder days, Barney Tuttle had ridden shotgun guard on Buck Pruitt's stage. And Barney still owned the sawed-off double-barreled Whitworth buckshot gun he had carried on the stage. It hung on the wall above Barney's bunk, and more than once Tap had held it in his hands, admiring it, while Barney told tales of those long past times. Barney kept the gun in perfect condition. The stock gleamed from endless rubbing, the barrel bores were mirrors of flawless polish, and the locks clicked with a velvety smoothness that told of perfect adjustment. On a shelf beside the gun was a partially filled box of brass-cased buckshot loads.

With Barney off somewhere, hobnobbing with some crony, Tap lifted down the gun, broke it open, and slid a pair of those brass-cased loads into the gaping chambers. Then, the gun at ready, he hurried back to Luke Casper's store.

It hadn't taken long, not over five minutes at the most, Tap figured. And now his heart was sure going it, forty to the dozen at least. Because the plain facts of the matter were, he was scared as hell! He just wasn't cut out to swap lead with anybody, let alone a real bad one like Nick Bodie. Yet he couldn't back away now. Because the inner force that had driven him against Chirk Dennis the other day, now had hold of him again, setting him against Nick Bodie.

Allie Langley came out of the Trading Post, market basket piled high with grocery supplies. Tap held back at the corner, waiting for her to get well past. And now, how to go about it? If Bodie was still inside, should he go root him out, or wait until he showed of his own accord?

Somebody, decided Tap dismally, with a better head than he had, or not as scared as he was, would know what to do, or at least have some idea how to handle the situation. But he didn't. Seemed all he could do was stand here and shake.

There was one grain of comfort. From all he had heard from Barney Tuttle and other oldtimers, there was something about a sawed-off buckshot gun that took all the salt and smoke out of the tough ones. Those gaping twin muzzles and what they spit out carried an awesome potency that even the meanest of the rough ones wanted no part of. Maybe it would work out that way now. Maybe Nick Bodie would cave and come along real peaceable . . .

So ran Tap Geer's thoughts as he waited, and so they ran as Nick Bodie stepped from the Trading Post door, paused at the head of the platform steps, and spun up a cigarette while surveying the street with seeming indifference.

Sure of himself, thought Tap bleakly — no matter what . . .

To Tap it was as though someone was behind him with a hand between his shoulders, pushing him into the clear past the corner of the building and past the end of the platform. As he moved, he drew back both hammers of the Whitworth gun, but soft as were their velvety clicks, the sound reached Bodie and he came swiftly half around. There he froze, and when he spoke, his words fell guttural and jerky.

"Now just what is this, Geer? Why the cannon? Who you gunning for?"

"You," returned Tap. "You — unless you

come down quietly and do as you're told. Come on off there, and keep your hands in sight!"

Nick Bodie started slowly down. "I still don't get this. Or is it that you figure to keep all of Sawbuck out of town forever? You got a long chore ahead if you do."

"This morning," said Tap, "early this morning, I saw you and Labine and Dennis down in the pothole country, turning Claymore beef over to Jett Chesbro. Since then, I've heard what happened to Indian Joe Ruiz. Right now Dave Howison and Milt Shannon are out at Sawbuck, rounding up Ben Walrode and the rest of his thieving gang. While me — I'm rounding up you. That's it, Bodie!"

Bodie paused, his face settling into a mask in which his eyes pinched down and down until they became mere glittering slits. He shrugged.

"I still can't figure this. But I'm not about to argue with that shotgun." He started on down but, in the next breath, threw himself off the far end of the steps, putting them between him and Tap.

In spite of all his care, the move caught Tap enough off guard so that when he turned loose a barrel of the Whitworth, with its booming report rolling down street, Nick Bodie had already dropped safely below the hail of buckshot. Tap was barely recovered from the recoil of the big gun when Bodie whirled out past the steps, his hand gun stabbing level.

This time Tap wasn't caught off guard. He turned loose the second barrel of the Whitworth and Nick Bodie was blasted off his feet as though by a hurricane wind.

Whitworth gun empty in his hands, Tap went slowly ahead, to stare for a moment at what lay crumpled just beyond the lower end of the steps. Quickly he turned away, dropped the Whitworth, leaned over Luke Casper's hitch rail, and was sick as a dog.

The day had about run out when Dave Howison left Basin City for home. He rode slowly, no shred of hurry left in him, as this had been one of the longest, most exhausting days of his life. Physical exertion, he decided somberly, was not the only thing that could take it out of a man; emotional drain could be far worse. And the iniquities of men, and the violence thus inevitably led to, could wipe the brightness from the best of days and lay a deep cloud of depression over the mind.

Almost, it seemed, these things must also leave some ugly effect on the very land itself, but as he looked across the wide run of the twilit basin ahead, he knew with a quick thankfulness that this was not so. The land was too big, too old, too secure, and men too impermanent with their stupid misdeeds and senseless miseries. The land would always be there, while men would not.

He came up a little straighter in the saddle, and as the miles slid back beneath the jogging hoofs of the buckskin, there was a lightening of his mood. And when those same hoofs splashed across Bannock Creek at the lower ford and turned upslope toward the light beckoning through night's early clotted darkness, a real edge of peace came to him. There ahead was home, and inside the security of its four walls a man might heal his thoughts and find full rest.

But not immediately this night. Woody Biggs was too full of demanding questions. Across the supper table Howison had to go over the entire day and its scarifying events. When he finished, Woody sat shaking a grizzled head.

"Hard to understand how Ben Walrode expected to get away with it. You'd think he'd know he was bound to be caught up with, one way or another."

Howison shrugged wearily. "Two lines of

thought make thieves out of men like Ben Walrode. Because of some flaw in their makeup, the mere idea of thievery appeals. And after that they see themselves as being much smarter than other men. To them, all other men are suckers, put on earth for the smart ones to make fools of."

Woody grunted. "They're the real fools. Today sure proved that. And if I was to say I was a bit sorry about Ben Walrode or them who worked with him, I'd be lying. Me, I'm sorry about Indian Joe Ruiz. And I'm sorry for Jock Dunaway. Losing a good rider and a real sizable gather of cattle is sure rough on the old boy."

"Jock will come out in pretty good shape," explained Howison soberly. "Once he got started, Chirk Dennis talked his head off. So, besides learning all about Ben Walrode's high and wild schemes, we heard of the money Jett Chesbro paid Jack Labine for the cattle. When Henry Kleyburg and Doc Church went out to Sawbuck after Walrode and Labine, they found the money in Walrode's desk. That goes to Jock, of course. And if it isn't enough, he's to take over some Sawbuck cattle to make up the difference. While Tap will make him a real fine hand, even better than the one he lost."

Woody exclaimed. "Tap Geer going to ride for Jock Dunaway?"

"That's right. He's ready to stay put on a job now and build a little future for himself. He couldn't find a better spot than with old Jock. Yeah, Tap grew up today, Woody. He had to, facing Nick Bodie."

Woody took a long drag at his coffee while considering this word. Then he nodded slowly. "Facing up to that kind of a showdown can sure straighten out any man's thinking. Even Milt Shannon's."

"There's a good man," said Howison quickly. "I wouldn't be sitting here right now, except for Milt Shannon. Walrode had me dead to rights, when Milt took care of him. Doc Church says he'll have Milt up and about before too long. When that happens, Milt Shannon is going to be my sheriff, all the way."

"Be set to take care of Jett Chesbro then, you think?"

Howison shook a thoughtful head. "Won't have to, Woody. We've seen the last of Jett Chesbro. The word of today and what happened is bound to get to him, and he'll know better than ever to show in these parts again. Somewhere else, he'll find a rustler's finish."

"The thieves, the crooks of all kinds —

they never learn," observed Woody philosophically. "Somewhere along the line they always pay up, full price. Playing it strictly honest, Ben Walrode could have done all right by himself. Maybe not quite as big as Henry Kleyburg or Miles Sulivane or Jock Dunaway, maybe. Though in time he could have been. But he just couldn't wait."

"Just couldn't wait," agreed Howison, nodding. "He had to try a short cut to easy beef and easy money."

Woody Biggs grunted again. "What he found was a short cut to hell!"

For the next two weeks, Howison never left his own land. With summer run out and the rougher seasons ahead, there was plenty of work to do, and he buried himself in it. But though this brought him a certain amount of mental and physical surcease, it wasn't enough. So came a day when he shaved and cleaned up and headed for the Kleyburg ranch.

It was a good day, keen and vigorous, full of the breath of autumn. A powder-blue haze lay all along the Cold River Rim and up and down the slopes of the Sentinels. Quail called plaintively from creek and river bank coverts, and once, from some great height, the clarion call of wild geese, winging south, came faintly down. A rising eagerness made Howison urge the big buckskin to a faster pace.

She was sitting on the deep veranda of the Kleyburg ranch house, busy over a bit of sewing, when Howison rode up. He was quickly out of the saddle, quickly up on the porch.

"Stay right there! Don't move!" he said.

She stared at him, startled. "What on earth . . . ?"

"I've been thinking how you'd look," he explained. "I always think of that, and when I see you, you never disappoint me. Always you look even better than I figured you might."

Color washed her cheeks. "The man," she told the world, a trifle shakily, "seems to be a bit daft. I don't understand him."

"Then I'll keep talking until you do." Howison hauled a chair up beside her. "Susie, what would you say if I told you the world for the rest of my life would be a pretty empty place unless you were riding with me?"

"Why," she answered, with a try at her old tartness, "I'd say I had to do considerable thinking on the matter." Even as she spoke, however, her glance turned very soft and a sober sweetness touched her lips. "Dad told all about — well, you know. It was pretty terrible, wasn't it? There are scars, David — inside?"

"There were," he told her. "But they heal fast when I sit here beside you. Girl, I asked you a question. How about a straight-out answer?"

For a breath or two she seemed passive, looking down at the sewing in her lap. Then her head came up and a glint of moisture misted her eyes.

"Like always, David, you talk me into a corner. But — but I'm so thankful that you do!"

She reached out and laid her hand in his.

The employees of Thorndike Press hope you have enjoyed this Large Print book. All our Thorndike and Wheeler Large Print titles are designed for easy reading, and all our books are made to last. Other Thorndike Press Large Print books are available at your library, through selected bookstores, or directly from us.

For information about titles, please call:

(800) 223-1244

or visit our Web site at:

www.gale.com/thorndike
www.gale.com/wheeler

To share your comments, please write:

Publisher
Thorndike Press
295 Kennedy Memorial Drive
Waterville, ME 04901